LEAVING
PROTECTION

LEAVING PROTECTION

Will Hobbs

📚 HarperCollins*Publishers*

Leaving Protection
Copyright © 2004 by Will Hobbs

Library of Congress Cataloging-in-Publication Data
Hobbs, Will.
Leaving Protection / by Will Hobbs.—1st ed.
p.   cm.
Summary: Sixteen-year-old Robbie Daniels, happy to get a job aboard a
troller fishing for king salmon off southeastern Alaska, finds himself in
danger when he discovers that his mysterious captain is searching for
long-buried Russian plaques that lay claim to Alaska and the Northwest.
ISBN 0-688-17475-2 — ISBN 0-06-051632-1 (lib. bdg.)
[1. Salmon fishing—Alaska—Fiction. 2. Buried treasure—Fiction.
3. Interpersonal relations—Fiction. 4. Alaska—Fiction.] I. Title.
PZ7.H6524Le 2004   2003015545
[Fic]—dc22

Typography by Larissa Lawrynenko
1 2 3 4 5 6 7 8 9 10
❖
First Edition

to Julie Yates and her father,
George Yates

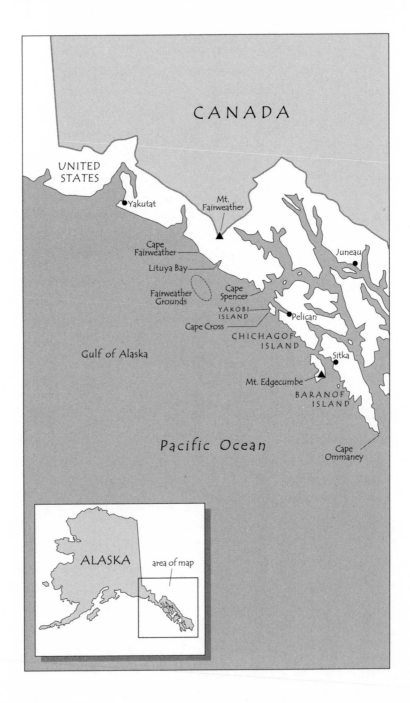

CANADA

UNITED
STATES

•Yakutat

Mt.
Fairweather

Juneau
•

Cape
Fairweather

Lituya Bay

Cape
Spencer

Fairweather
Grounds

YAKOBI
ISLAND

•Pelican

Cape Cross

CHICHAGOF
ISLAND

•Sitka

Gulf of Alaska

Mt. Edgecumbe

BARANOF
ISLAND

Pacific Ocean

Cape
Ommaney

ALASKA   area of map

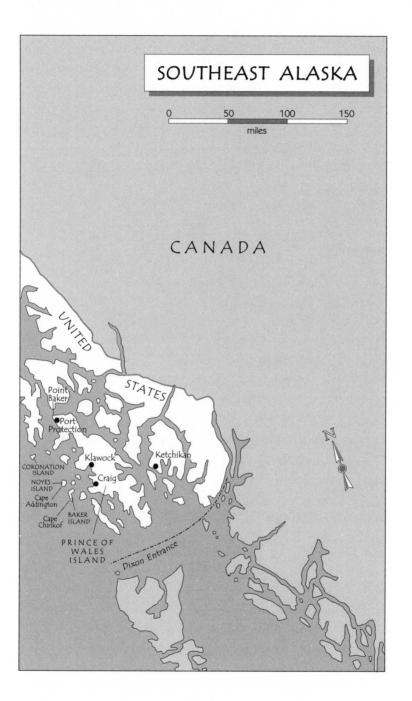

SOUTHEAST ALASKA

0   50   100   150
miles

CANADA

UNITED

STATES

Point
Baker
●Port
Protection

CORONATION
ISLAND

NOYES
ISLAND

Cape
Addington

Cape
Chirikof

BAKER
ISLAND

Klawock ●

● Craig

Ketchikan ●

N

PRINCE OF
WALES
ISLAND

Dixon Entrance

LEAVING
PROTECTION

1

STRANGE, HOW IT ALL BEGAN. Silence hung over breakfast like a spell. Somebody would make an attempt at cheerful conversation and then it would die out like a campfire built with wet wood.

I kept straining for the sound of an airplane motor. My parents and my little sister were doing the same. Maddie, who was ten, was sneaking glances like she might never see me again. My parents were in favor of my plan but they were nervous, too. If everything worked out, I was going to work on a boat fishing the outside waters.

We live in a house that goes up and down with the tides, which are huge in southeast Alaska. We live in the inside waters, in a small cove in Port Protection's back bay. Protection is up in the northern tip of Prince of Wales Island, the biggest of the eleven hundred islands in the panhandle of Alaska, or "Southeast," as we call it.

Port Protection is little, and by little I mean tiny. No streets, no cars, one store. We've got more boats than we do people.

I was born in our floathouse, and so was Maddie. The moss-covered house and the hodgepodge of cables engineered to let it ride up and down with the tides look like something Dr. Seuss thought up, but my parents get all the credit. One big cedar tree from the mountainside behind us provided all the lumber and the shingle siding. The rusty metal roof is secondhand and so are the single-pane windows, which leak lots of heat. Almost always, there's a fire burning in the stove. Our clothes smell like woodsmoke, but they're clean. We're rich in a lot of ways, but money isn't one of them.

To make some cash money, that's why I was leaving Protection.

"You don't have to go," Maddie said, breaking the silence.

"But I want to," I told her. "I'm so excited I can't stand it. I've been waiting to do this for years."

"We need you on *our* boat," she insisted.

My parents, who knew better, were sitting this one out. "You guys will do fine without me for a few weeks," I said.

"Just because you're sixteen now, and old enough

to get a deckhand license—that doesn't mean it's a good idea, Robbie."

I reached over and gave my sister a hug. Just then the whole house pitched up. Books and nicknacks went flying off the shelves, and the sugar bowl sailed across the breakfast table. My father reached out and tried to grab it but missed. When it crashed to the floor, the pieces of china went everywhere.

Quick as can be, a smile replaced my mother's alarm. "Humpback," she announced. We ran outside onto the deck just as the behemoth's broad back gracefully broke the surface only feet away. The whale blew out its pipes as it passed alongside our salmon troller, which was moored at the dock. The spout took its time dissolving into the morning mist.

By now we'd figured out what the whale had been doing under our feet: rubbing off barnacles against the big logs that float the house. It had happened only once before, when Maddie was too young to remember. "It's a good sign for Robbie fishing the big water," my sister cried. My parents nodded like they thought so, too, but it crossed my mind that it could be just the opposite. Not that I'm superstitious exactly, but when you've grown up around the corner from the Gulf of Alaska, you've seen some of what Mother Nature can do.

Right about then we heard the floatplane. A minute later Moose Borden was tipping his wing at us as he zoomed over the back bay. He landed out of sight but was soon motoring up to the house to get me. I'd been ready the day before, but I had to wait until

3

Borden had a paying passenger to drop off at Port Protection. Moose was a family friend, and my flight was going to be free of charge.

Good-byes were brief. "Keep your eye out for a glass fishing float for me," my sister said.

"Definitely," I told her.

"Heads up out there on the ocean," my father cautioned. "Stay focused."

"You better believe I will," I promised.

My mother flashed a confident smile. "Catch a ton of kings, Robbie."

And that was pretty much it. I grabbed my stuff and a couple minutes later I was flying over the floathouse. My family was looking up and waving like there was no tomorrow.

2

I WAS ON MY WAY TO CRAIG, about halfway down
Prince of Wales Island, fifty or so air miles. Craig is
one of the major fishing towns in Southeast, and the
metropolis of the island with around fourteen hundred
people. It was a short hop by air taxi, and I spent it fret-
ting. The July 1 opening of king salmon season was
less than forty-eight hours away. I only hoped I hadn't
cut it too close.

My first glimpse of Craig's harbor, out the window
of the floatplane, had me doubting my chances of landing a job. The docks were crawling with fishermen,
and this late in the game, skippers were unlikely to be
hiring crew. But I could still get lucky.

Moose splashed down, taxied toward the floatplane

dock, throttled back, then killed the motor at the precise moment that would allow the airplane's momentum to drift it to within stepping distance of the dock.

When Moose jumped off and tied up, I was right behind him. I thanked him for the huge favor, slung my daypack onto my back, grabbed my duffel bag, and took off running.

The boat harbor was only a couple of blocks away. I slowed down as I got to the parking lot and stopped to catch my breath, feasting my eyes on the forest of masts, trolling poles, antennas, and exhaust stacks below: fishing boats, nearly all of them. I would settle for a gill-netter or a seiner, and happily pocket my wages, but catching fish with nets wasn't really what I was after. A troller was what I was shooting for. There's no other fishing that compares.

I started down the ramp to the docks. The tide was out, so the ramp was steep. It was busy with people going down, hands full of gear and groceries, and people coming back up, hands empty.

At the bottom, I took a right on the dock's first side branch to see what the eagles were screaming about. The commotion was coming from the lawn of a house in the lap of the marina. A dozen or so bald eagles were fighting over some fish guts someone had thrown on the grass, maybe the white-haired man looking out the picture window.

Just like our chickens back home with their scraps, the eagles were running in all directions with their prizes, fighting off the ones who had dropped theirs the moment they suspected that the other guy had a superior tangle of guts. They ran so stiff-legged, throwing their weight from side to side, it was almost comical.

Someone was watching me watch the eagles. A voice passing by my shoulder said, "It's a dog-eat-dog world out there." It was a woman's voice, infectiously friendly. With a glance I recognized her as an island legend, a teacher from Craig who had fished the outside waters with her father since she was a small girl.

She paused, a plastic laundry tub full of canned goods on her hip and a boy about ten in tow. Her hair was long and jet black. Like me, she was part native— Haida, in her case. She had a big friendly smile on her face.

I was tongue-tied. Her father's power troller, the *Julie Kristine*, famously named after her, was in the very next slip. "You're not from around here," she said.

"Port Protection," I replied. "You're George Yates's daughter, right?"

"You bet," she said with a grin.

"I saw an article about you in the *Island News* a couple of months ago. About how you took kids canoeing on the Thorne River."

"Amazingly, they all got back alive. Do you homeschool, or go to school in Protection?"

"We used to homeschool, but the last three or four years I've been taking our motorboat in to the public school."

"I'm glad you're helping to keep it open. How

many kids are enrolled these days?"

"Nineteen, first grade through high school."

Her son was tugging at her sleeve. She gave him a sharp glance and he quit tugging. She patted him on the head as she explained, "Bear thinks the season will get here sooner if he gets even more excited. It's his first king season."

"I'll run ahead and help Grampa," Bear said, and took off. His mother set her things down. "So where are you headed with that duffel bag?" she asked.

When I told her about my situation, Julie was doubtful about my plans. It wasn't so much that all the jobs had been taken, as she explained. With the price of salmon down drastically for the third straight year, crewing had become a dicey proposition. A lot of the local college and high school kids thought anything else, even working in a video store or delivering pizzas, was a better bet.

"It's a real shame," she said. "I put myself all the way through college crewing on my dad's boat. Some people say kids aren't fishing because the work is too hard, but I think it's because they've done their math. Fifteen percent of the captain's paycheck isn't so attractive these days. Your own overhead is going to run you, let's see, for starters, sixty dollars for your crew license."

"I brought the money. And my ID."

"Okay, factor in your share of the groceries, which will come out of your earnings. The season might run two weeks, and groceries are expensive.

So's the captain's fuel, and a percentage of that might be yours."

"I have to pay part of the fuel?"

"With some skippers you do, with some you don't. It gets subtracted from your take, same as the food. Add it all up, you could be starting out a couple hundred dollars in the hole, maybe more. If your captain doesn't catch many fish, you could end up owing *him* money."

"You're kidding."

She shook her head. "I wish I was."

"Well then," I said, "at least there must be a lot of jobs available."

"Not really. A lot of skippers can't afford a deckhand. Lots of them are working alone."

"That's dangerous."

"Absolutely."

"Come on, there has to be *some* money to be made. The quota is decent this year, right?"

"A hundred and sixty thousand kings for Southeast, but who knows where they're going to be? Some boats don't get within a hundred miles of where the big numbers are being caught. The season could be over before you start making money. I've known it to close in six days. Look, I hate to sound so discouraging. What do you think? Do you still want to try to find a boat?"

"I don't have a video store to work at in Protection, and there sure isn't any work up there delivering pizzas."

Maybe it was the way I'd said it. She laughed even

though she knew it wasn't funny. "I've been waiting my whole life to turn sixteen so I could do this," I explained. "I gotta find a highliner."

We both knew I was in the company of a highliner at that very moment. The *Julie Kristine* was one of those trollers known to return from the outside waters half-sunk with fish, time after time. Julie and her dad were true highliners. Not that they would use that term to describe themselves, not in a million years. It's always the other guy who's the highliner.

"Got any you could recommend to me?" I asked her.

"A highliner, eh? There aren't many to begin with, and they tend to have the same person working with them year after year. Someone who knows their every move and works at least as hard as they do."

I was thinking as fast as I could. "What about a boat from out of state?" I said. "A boat from Washington, maybe?"

"Hey, good idea. Maybe you could talk to the buyer over at Craig Fish. Ask if he knows a big-time producer who usually fishes solo."

"I guess that would be a long shot."

"Wait a minute," Julie said. "I just thought of a guy who matches your description. He comes up every summer. I saw him pull in yesterday. He's been fishing even longer than my dad. When you're out on the drag, every time you look over at that man, he's pulling fish."

"Now you're talking. This is perfect. I could work

on a troller! That was what I was hoping."

"Hey, don't get carried away. I don't even know this guy. All I know about him is, he catches a lot of fish. Chances are he won't hire a deckhand. Those old-timers are set in their ways, and he's used to fishing alone."

"I feel lucky," I told her. "I want to give him a try. What's the name of my boat?"

"The *Storm Petrel*, out of Port Angeles, Washington."

"Keep an eye out for me on the drag," I said. "And thanks."

"I'll wave," she said.

3

ALL THE WAY DOWN THE dock and on the left, in the last slip, that's where I found the *Storm Petrel* moored. It was a salmon troller to die for, forty-five feet or so, with a fiberglass hull. She was white with green trim and immaculately maintained. As I approached I kept an eye out for my Washington State highliner.

Through the wraparound windows of the wheelhouse, I could see the little table where the skipper ate his meals, and behind it, the galley with his stove and sink. On the opposite side, behind the wheel, was his bunk. He wasn't inside. Along the slip, I walked the length of the troller. I didn't find him on the deck behind the wheelhouse or in the cockpit along the back of the boat. He must have walked up to the grocery store, I figured.

A highliner was worth waiting for.

I waited, got restless, then committed a cardinal sin. With a guilty glance along the dock to see if anyone was looking, I stepped over the bulwark. The hardwood trim was exquisite, with not so much as a varnish bubble showing. I walked across the *Storm Petrel*'s bright turquoise green deck, leaned on the hayrack, and admired the fish-cleaning cradles in the holding bins on either side of the boat. Each of the cradles—simple, V-shaped plywood devices for keeping a salmon spine-down as you clean it—had a fish gaff lying in it, at the ready. Wouldn't that be something, to be standing in the cockpit of a boat as splendid as this one, hauling huge kings aboard!

With another glance over my shoulder—the coast was clear—I swung down into the cockpit. My hand on a gurdy lever, I imagined I was pulling the gear up, a king salmon on every hook. I grabbed the fish gaff, leaned over the stern, and pretended I was clubbing, then gaffing, a huge king. With the king landed in the cleaning bin, at least in my imagination, I returned the gaff to the exact position where I'd found it.

No one was watching, so I snooped around a little more. Here was a small wheel, just like on my family's boat, so you could steer from the stern as well as from inside the wheelhouse. Here was a remote station for the autopilot; we had that, too. Barely forward of the cockpit, dead center and waist high, was an enclosure of painted hardboard open only to the back, to keep a few things accessible yet out of the rain. I spotted a plastic tray full of lures. With a peek around, I reached for it. I found hootchies of various colors, their wavy plastic tentacles concealing number seven Mustad hooks that the fisherman had filed extra sharp. Off to the side, brass spoons were soaking in a bucket of Hydrotone so they wouldn't tarnish.

I was about to put the lure tray back when something caught my eye, the dull dark plate of metal that the tray had been sitting on. It had a strange sort of emblem on it.

I set the tray aside and reached for the metal plate. Rectangular, about eight by ten—whatever it was, it was heavy. The metal was copper, badly tarnished. Or was it some kind of alloy? The emblem, under the number 13, was a two-headed eagle with its wings spread wide. The heads faced in opposite directions. I'd seen a figure like it on a totem pole once. The plate looked really old, and there was writing across the bottom in a strange alphabet.

"Looking for something?" came a voice like a thunderclap. I jumped, turned around, shrank back. Right above me, filling up the sky in an old gray halibut coat, was a very angry fisherman. My heart went to jackhammering as I set the strange metal plate back where I'd found it.

"What are you doing on my boat?" the man demanded, the captain of the *Storm Petrel* no doubt, big as a Sitka spruce, with a long, angular face furrowed by the weather, a full head of gray hair, and an untrimmed salt-and-pepper beard. His dark eyes, sharp as his hooks, were easy enough to read. He had me dead to rights, and he was thinking of skinning me alive.

"I'm really sorry," I said.

He scowled at me like I was the ugliest bottom feeder he'd seen in his life. My eyes went to his massive forearms. I think of myself as plenty sturdy, but his fish-killing hands could have reached down and throttled my neck like a chicken's.

"'Sorry'?" he boomed.

I scrambled out of the cockpit and got the heck off his boat. On the pier, I reached for my stuff, but the fisherman stepped in front of me, blocking my way. "Where do you think you're going?"

I took a step back. "I knew better," I said, afraid to look into his face. "Really, I apologize. I don't blame you for being mad."

"*You* don't blame *me*?"

"Just let me go."

I watched closely to see if he was going to kill me, or have a heart attack, or what. His eyes were bulging like a red snapper's when it's yanked to the surface.

He was livid, but at the same time, he seemed to be wrestling to get himself under control, which I was all in favor of.

His eyes went disapprovingly to the small gold

hoop on my right ear. "I want to know who you are and what you were looking for."

All I could think of to say was the simple truth: "I was looking for a boat."

"This one's not for sale," he shot back.

"I mean, I want to *work* on a boat," I explained.

"You've got a strange way of going about it."

"I know. I know I've blown it." This sorehead was never going to let me off the hook. "I feel awful," I said. "Especially because I didn't want to work on just any boat, I wanted to work on yours. I got all excited about the idea, came on board, and got carried away."

His overgrown eyebrows lifted. "Why *my* boat?"

"Because George Yates's daughter recommended you."

"Who?"

"Julie Kristine. She's a teacher who fishes with her father every summer."

"I don't know her."

"I'm not from around here. She is. Maybe you've seen the boat named after her."

"I'm thinking I have. Did she send you to snoop around my boat?"

"Why would she do that?"

The captain of the *Storm Petrel* hesitated, cast a glance back toward the cockpit, then said nothing. He just looked me up and down, his eyes full of suspicion.

"She just recommended you," I tried to assure him. "Like I said, she told me you're one of the best."

He settled down a little. "Keep talking."

"She says you've got a fish-catching boat, and a fish-catching boat is what I'm looking for."

"Didn't she tell you I work alone?"

"She did. I just wanted to hear it from you."

"I work alone. There, I've said it."

I'd dug myself a huge hole, but maybe I would get lucky and climb out of it. He had the charm of a wolf eel, but he was a highliner, the real article.

I started pedaling as fast as I could. "My name's Robbie Daniels," I began. "I won't get in your way, I won't talk if you don't want me to, I'll work like you wouldn't believe. I just want the chance to work. I'll work as hard as you do, even harder."

The highliner squinted at me. Maybe he was interested. I started talking even faster. "I'll get up as soon as you do. I'll work all the hours you do. I don't care about breaks. I'll do the dishes, I'll clean fish as long as there's daylight, I'll do all the work down in the fish hold, I'll take over the wheel if you want to catch a nap—"

The fisherman lifted his huge paw, indicating I should stop. "Robbie Daniels, you said your name was?"

"Yes sir."

"Just get out of here," the highliner said abruptly.

I can't say I left with my head held high. I might have been relieved if I hadn't been so disgusted. Not with him, but with myself.

4

IT WAS ALL I COULD DO to not give up right then and there. Part of me wanted to get back home to Protection as fast as possible. If I hurried, my pilot might still be over at the floatplane dock.

Moose Borden was going to think I was nuts. I could hear him saying, "How many skippers did you talk to, Robbie?"

I told myself to calm down, start over, and try again. That's what I did. I worked it hard all around the docks. It turned out just like the teacher had thought: skippers couldn't afford a deckhand, or they'd already hired one. Half a dozen had hired only the day before.

By four in the afternoon I was ready to give up, and I was starving. I found a chowder place nearby and

ordered a halibut burger with curly fries and a chocolate malt. The place was noisy, packed with fishermen
counting down the hours as they swapped tales and
talked king salmon gear, the weather, and their
chances. They were already dressed in their fishing
jeans, Carhartts like mine. Being this close to the
Super Bowl of commercial fishing in Southeast, and
knowing I wasn't going to get in on the game, there
was a gnawing hunger in my gut that food couldn't
touch. When my burger arrived, I started in, but I
couldn't even taste it.

It felt like I was the only one sitting alone, but I
wasn't. Over in the far corner, an old-timer turned
around and gave me a long, pained look. It was the captain of the *Storm Petrel*, his face as unforgiving as the
ocean.

I turned my attention to my burger and my
thoughts to the family friends I would be staying with
that night. It was time I should be checking in with
them. Too bad they didn't know a boat I could work
on; my parents had already asked.

I wanted to dump my stuff at their house so I
wouldn't have to lug it around with me. Then I'd make
one last round of the boats. There had been quite a few
with nobody aboard when I'd been job hunting.

Without a backward glance toward the captain of
the *Petrel*, I left the restaurant and headed for the pay
phone around the corner of the building. I'd dropped
two quarters and was punching numbers when someone crowded in behind me. I looked up, and it was the

captain of the *Storm Petrel*. "Put down that phone," he said.

Did he think he owned me after one dumb mistake? "How come?" I said. It's not like I hadn't already apologized. If he wasn't going to let it drop, I was ready to stand up for myself.

Just as a voice came over the phone, the fisherman reached out and disconnected me. "Look," he said, his voice softening suddenly, his eyes, too, "I shouldn't have jumped all over you the way I did."

I was so surprised. Now it was the highliner who was apologizing, and he sounded sincere despite the rough edges. "That's okay," I said. "I had it coming."

"So, you're looking for a boat. Or did you find one?"

"No sir, I'm afraid I haven't."

"Grab your stuff and come back to my troller. We'll talk about it, if you're still interested."

This was almost too good to be true. "Sure, let's talk," I said. "I don't want to miss king season if I can help it."

We started walking. "You were going on about what a hard worker you are," the old-timer said on our way back along the dock. "What kind of experience you got?"

"Tons. I was raised on a salmon troller."

"A fisherman born and raised, eh? I suppose you know all about GPS navigation, how to read the nautical charts, the Fathometer, the radar."

"All that."

He stopped in his tracks. The slightest of grins was remaking his face into a shape that was refreshingly human. "What is it you *won't* do, tell me that."

Here was my chance to let him know there was something I wanted out of this besides money. I said, "I won't not pull the salmon."

"Huh?"

"I mean, I want to catch fish myself, whenever I'm caught up with the cleaning and icing. If you have to work all four lines and land all the fish by yourself, I'm not interested."

He seemed amused. "You're pretty firm on that, I take it."

"That's right. I want to be conking kings and pulling as many aboard as I can."

"Fish till your arms fall off, it sounds like."

Finally we were talking the same language. "That's right," I said. "I've always wanted this kind of a chance. *Chimes of Freedom*, my family's boat, is only twenty-eight feet long. Where we fish, there aren't many kings. There's nothing in the world like having a big king salmon on your hands."

"Tell me about that," the fisherman said. His dark eyes, green as the north Pacific a fathom below the surface, betrayed a fisherman's fondness for the subject at hand. This was more like it.

I emptied the whole bucket: "Once you take that leader off the trolling wire and it's just you and the king, no fishing pole, just the line in your hands and the hook in its jaw and all that power running through the line, through your hands, all the way down your spine, you feel as connected as you're ever going to get."

"Connected to what?" he asked.

"Connected to . . . everything."

He nodded thoughtfully, then started walking along the dock again. "You drink coffee?" he asked as we reached the *Storm Petrel*. His tone of voice was downright civil.

Maybe I'd said the right things. Maybe he did have the need for a good deckhand. "If you got a big slug of sugar to put in it," I said.

"So, you like a little coffee with your sugar. You must be a Turk."

The guy was actually loosening up. "I'm not Turkish," I said with a grin, "but I am one-eighth Tlingit, on my father's side."

"Did he raise you Tlingit?"

"No, and he didn't grow up native either. I've learned some stuff out of books, but that hardly counts. The Tlingits are the Indians that the Russians stole southeast Alaska from."

"The Russian fur hunters were a scurvy lot. Barbarians."

"Hey, watch it," I shot back. "I'm part Russian, too."

He laughed, actually laughed, then led me onto his boat and into the wheelhouse. I was thinking about that metal plate: a Tlingit symbol over Russian words, was my guess, not that I was going to press my luck and bring it up.

"Part what else are you, then?" the highliner asked as he took two big mugs from the cup hooks above his galley stove. They were wide and squat, with traction pads to resist the pull of heavy seas in the open ocean. He set them on the rail between the stove and the little dining table. "German, English, Norwegian, and Irish," I answered.

"What a coincidence," he said as he poured a brew dark like old engine oil into the mugs. "Those last two, that's me. My father was a gloomy Norseman and my ma was Irish, a tempest in a teapot. The part in me that riles easy, I blame it on her."

I sat down at his table. As he settled in across from me, the fisherman reached for a big bottle of extra-strength Tylenol and shook out three capsules. He washed them down with coffee.

"Sounds like you're not from Klawock, the Tlingit town," he continued. "And we already established that you're not from Craig."

"I'm from way up at Port Protection. You know where that is?"

"Sure, I know Protection. I knew it from when it was just the summer fish plant and the trading post. You live along the boardwalk?"

"No, in the back bay, in a floathouse."

"No kidding. Up and down with the tide. They ever punch in one of those logging roads?"

"Every so often there's talk, but the locals, including

my parents, like it the way it is. It would be the end of our big trees."

"And a whole lot more. Are you a subsistence family?"

"Yep, we're still in the hunter-gatherer stage, rounding up our food as best we can. We've got our shrimp pots, crab pots, greenhouse, and our salmon troller, the *Chimes of Freedom*. We salvage stuff and turn it into something else."

"Self-reliance people."

"You could say that. My parents came to Protection a long time ago to live away from the power grid."

"You must have a generator."

"We only use ours for backup these days. My sister hated it when she couldn't hear the whales spouting. There's a creek right behind us. My dad and I built a setup where the creek turns a paddle wheel on a crankshaft that works a pulley attached to an alternator."

"Not too shabby. Can you store the juice for when you have a heavy load?"

"In a bank of eight twelve-volt batteries. The microwave especially draws a lot of juice."

"You're all set up, then."

"We get by. I can't make any money there, that's the problem."

"Your father's got a salmon troller, but he doesn't do any serious commercial fishing? Why can't he pay you to keep working on the family boat?"

"We fish the other four species of salmon, but the

only real money these days is in the kings, and we can't get to them. Boat's not big enough. Even when the kings are in the inside water, they're running deeper than we can fish. Those lighter cannonballs only take the gear down fifteen fathoms, twenty at the most."

"Wait a second, you aren't *hand* trollers, are you?"

The guy was back to looking at me like I was some kind of bottom feeder. "Yep," I admitted, "we crank our lines by hand."

"In that case you've got no experience to run my power gurdies."

"I've run 'em some on other people's boats."

"Some?" he asked skeptically.

"You're right. I won't get your lines up and down as fast as you, at least not at first."

He didn't say anything. I was about finished with my coffee, and it looked like my highliner was about finished with me. He'd only wanted to make himself feel better about the way he'd acted when he caught me on his boat. No hard feelings, have a good life.

The clock above the table said a quarter to six. Last chance to track down a few more skippers to talk to. I got up to go.

"Slow down," the highliner said irritably. "Something you said earlier this afternoon made me think."

"What was that?"

"It was about you doing everything in the hold. Icing the fish and all. I've been having some trouble with my back, quite a bit of trouble."

I waited for him to go on.

"It's been seizing up on me for years. It comes and goes, but I've always been able to work through it. Last summer it got real bad for a spell. Climbing in and out of the hold, all that stoop work down there . . . if it got even worse—"

"I'm your man," I said.

"I can't tell you how long it's been since I had a deckhand," he said. "And I've never had one that worked out."

"This time will be different."

"It better be. I expect you to make good on all those things you said."

"I guarantee it."

"Fifteen percent and half of the grub and the fuel? Is that still the way it works?"

Rather than quibble, I said, "It works for me."

"Tor Torsen," he said, extending his hand across the table. "Call me Tor."

"Good deal, Tor. What time should I report tomorrow?"

"Tomorrow?" he said incredulously. "You expect to hop on at the last second, after all the prep work is done? Icing the hold and so on?"

"I didn't mean it like that. I mean, I was going to stay in Craig tonight with some friends of my family. That's who I was going to call. They just moved down from Protection."

"Hey, sleep on the boat. I aim to put you to work.

We have a lot of grocery shopping to do; we could be out for a couple of weeks. And there's leaders to rig. I suppose you know how to do that."

"Sure, sure."

"Call those people—be quick about it. Tell 'em you aren't coming. Just throw your stuff aboard. I'll be waiting when you come back."

"Good deal," I said, a little uncertainly. I didn't really understand how all this had happened. I had a strange feeling, like I was being flooded by a high tide. I wished I had more time to think, but this was my big chance. I was going to have to take it or leave it.

I took it.

5

WE PULLED OUT OF CRAIG at six the next evening. I sat on the aft deck, on the big hatch lid over the fish hold, watching the harbor recede. The houses on the hill grew smaller and the clearcuts on Sunnahae Mountain grew large. After a fast-moving rain, everything was golden in the evening light.

There was no telling how long I might be out on the ocean. If king season stayed open for two weeks, Tor wasn't going to lose time resupplying in the middle of it. The galley pantry was stocked to the gills with canned goods, plus we had four milk crates overflowing with refrigerated stuff. Like the *Chimes*, the *Storm Petrel* had no refrigerator. The fish hold was one big icebox. Push back the hatch lid and the milk crates were right there, on a tray spanning the pit.

Torsen wove his way among the outer islands for several hours. It was obvious he knew these waters as well as any local skipper. He dropped anchor in Pigeon Pass. The anchorage was in the lee of Baker Island, out of reach of the swells coming off the open ocean. My highliner lay down on his bunk behind the wheel just after nine. A couple of minutes, no more, and he was sawing logs. I hung out on the deck listening to the spouting of nearby whales, rehearsing what it would be like to run the power gurdies.

The sea swallowed the sun around ten. It was after eleven before the lights atop the masts of the surrounding trollers were shining bright. Summer days in Alaska, how they linger. Locals like me hate to waste precious daylight. Sleep is for winter, when you're not missing anything but darkness.

Come morning, my family would be fishing in the Sumner Strait, without me. After all these years, that was going to be strange for all of us. One thing we'd agreed on—especially since we couldn't be in touch: No worrying!

It was nearly dark as I made my way past Torsen's bunk and eased down the ladder to my own bed in the nose of the troller, the fo'c'sle. As I got horizontal, images from the last two days played across my mind until I was picturing the metal plate, the old plaque or whatever it was, I had been handling when Tor surprised me in the cockpit. Before the double-headed eagle even came into focus, I fell into a chasm of sleep.

Next thing I knew, the engine was rumbling to life.

A troller's motor firing up will get your attention when you're sleeping a few yards away from it, but the anchor being pulled jars you on a whole other scale. Picture being crammed in a small metal garbage can being beaten on by lunatics with tire irons. That's the effect of the anchor chain passing through its roller on the bow just a few feet above your head.

Before my mind switched on, I assumed I was on my family's boat. But the engine was more powerful and the rattle of the chain wasn't the same. The dark shape on the opposite bunk was my duffel bag and not my sister. Then I remembered. I had taken a job on a troller called the *Storm Petrel*, and my first shot at king season was about to begin.

I threw on my clothes and my rubber boots, grabbed my jacket and wool cap, and raced up the ladder. Torsen had returned from the bow and was lowering the trolling pole on the starboard side to its fishing position, at a forty-five-degree angle. The *Storm Petrel*'s poles were about forty feet long. Not waiting to be told, I lowered the port pole, then dropped the port stabilizer into the water a few seconds after he'd dropped his. It was a quarter to four, and dawn was already under way over the mountains of the islands between us and Prince of Wales. By the dim light, I could see some of the other captains pulling anchor.

In Torsen's wake, I returned to the warmth of the wheelhouse. For a big man and an old-timer, Tor moved fast. In seconds he fixed himself a mug of instant coffee, gave it a good stir, jammed a powdered donut into his mouth, and slid into his captain's chair behind the wheel. With his free hand he put the *Storm Petrel* in gear and we were rolling. "Leth's guh fithing," he said through his donut. He motioned with his chin for me to help myself to the open box.

Just like on the *Chimes*, the galley stove was set to 350 degrees around the clock, which was how the wheelhouse stayed warm and the ever-present pot of water stayed hot. As I might have guessed, Torsen didn't fool with brewing coffee when he was fishing. He'd bought eight tins of presweetened instant, and had started in on the mocha. I thought about hot chocolate but went with the mocha coffee. I wished I hadn't stayed up late. It wasn't so smart to be starting out with a major sleep deficit.

At the table, I drowsily dunked donuts and slurped coffee as I looked over the bow at the swells we were approaching. During the brief dark hours, a front had kicked in from the southwest. To the east, the dawn was cloud-riddled and promising to be spectacular. The times I had been on the outside waters with my family—I could count them on one hand—were during freakish periods of flat calm. We would never have ventured out on a day like this with our smaller boat.

When the *Petrel* hit the first swells, its bow began to rise dramatically and I could feel them rolling under the length of the boat. It was a rush, especially when I thought about the seas that might lie ahead in the coming hours and days.

It wasn't like I'd never seen swells or bad weather, or gone through any scrapes on the inside water. It's just that once you're outside, the stakes are a lot higher. There are no islands out there to knock down the power of the sea. There's nothing to hide behind. You ride it out or you run for cover.

All my life I knew I would go to sea one day, with all its dangers. And here I was.

I went out onto the deck with my mug and donut and watched the dawn unfold. Gulls and kittiwakes were diving and screaming in the *Petrel*'s wake. The face of every ripple on the sea was lit with a brush stroke of vermilion. The other boats from Pigeon Pass fell in behind us, single file, trolling poles at the ready.

Back inside the wheelhouse, I watched the instrument monitors as the captain steered around a rocky point and started south. We entered Veta Bay along the fifty-fathom contour, which meant we were three hundred feet off the bottom. Underwater pinnacles, marked by stars on the GPS monitor, had to be avoided. Drag your fishing gear over them, you lose the gear.

"Whales port and starboard," I said.

My highliner nodded gravely. "Good indicators. They're feeding on herring and needlefish, same as our kings. Lots of birds around, too. Look, a couple miles ahead—they're swarming over a big patch of feed."

I had to squint to make out the swarm. "Is the

weather building?" I asked. I wasn't ready to be tested with big water this soon.

"Not necessarily."

The skipper switched to autopilot, then reached for his heavy rubberized rain bottoms. I started pulling my own on. This didn't mean rain from the sky. It meant, if we were lucky, blood and slime from the sea.

The bib-type bottoms reach to your chest and fasten with suspenders. Torsen threw me a pair of blue rubber gloves from the cabinet above the fire extinguisher, then pulled on a pair of his own. "This is it," he said. "You wait all year for this."

"I've waited my whole life."

"So let's get after 'em, kid!"

I followed Tor past the fish-hold hatch. We parted company at the hayrack, the assembly of galvanized pipe that horseshoed around the machinery and instruments at the rear center of the boat. The hayrack is about five feet above the deck and a good thing to hang on to when you're moving around the back of the troller.

When I saw Tor was headed left, I swung right. Hand on the hayrack, I stepped through the cleaning bin and dropped into the cockpit, the waist-high well along the very back of the boat where the work of the fishing is done. I couldn't help taking a quick glance around, hoping to spot the plaque with the double-headed eagle, but it was nowhere to be seen.

Tor had the spreads at the ready in the tray underneath the hardwood rail around the stern. There were eleven for each of the two trolling lines on my side of the boat. Each of the spreads was a dozen or so feet of hundred-pound-test monofilament leader with the lure on the business end. On the other end was a snap for attaching the leader to the fishing line, which was made of braided stainless steel wire.

I ran the two lines down on my side, he ran his down, and then we waited. Once the thin steel fishing lines were spooled off the gurdy reels, we ran them out to be supported by the trolling poles. We were fishing down to thirty-two fathoms, at a trolling speed of 3.2 knots, a little less than four miles an hour. Keeping a close eye on the cockpit Fathometer and making small adjustments with the cockpit autopilot, the skipper was steering a course over a forty-three-fathom bottom.

Behind us, we were trailing forty-four lures. A third were big brass spoons and two-thirds were hootchies, plastic squid with waving tentacles kind of like hula skirts. The spreads with hootchies were rigged with a big orange flasher three feet up from the lure. The flashers, orange with a reflecting strip down the middle, have a crazy action in the water. With thirty doing their thing, the effect is like a marching band. Hey there, come to the parade, tasty snacks everywhere you look!

We might have waited two minutes, no more than it took for me to be distracted by a whale off the port side.

"Tip!" exclaimed Tor. My eyes shot to the line that

attached to the tip of his trolling pole. Nothing was going on. Then it occurred to me to look at my own pole. My tip line was jerking frantically. This was definitely a king.

"You tell me when," I cried.

"Give it about one minute," Tor replied. "Some of his friends might get jealous."

The heavy, the closer line that was weighed down by the heavier cannonball, was jerking, too. So, I noticed, were both of the skipper's lines.

"The bite is on!" Tor declared. "Bring 'em up, Robbie!"

6

HURRIED TO RETRIEVE THE upper spreads on my outside line. I snapped four of them onto the wire in the
gear tray, slapping the flashers or spoons along the
waist-high rail on my side of the back of the boat.

Right hand on the gurdy lever, I brought the line up
some more. I could see into the depths only as far as
two more empty hooks, one a spoon and one a
hootchie behind a flasher. Then suddenly there came a
flash of silver, a large twisting king salmon on the sev-
enth spread.

As I got the sixth spread out of the way, my first
king leaped clean out of the ocean. It was not only a
king, it was a *big* king.

"Yes sir!" Tor called. Nothing like fish, I thought, to make a highliner sing. I caught the motion of the big man on my left swinging his gaff, and I heard a dull thud as it connected. A king salmon, in a blurred arc, flew out of the ocean and into the cleaning bin on his side of the stern.

As I unsnapped the leader with my prize only twelve feet away, it streaked back and forth, down and up, and then, like a torpedo, charged underneath the boat. For my money there's not a more elegantly designed swimmer in the sea than the king salmon, a.k.a. chinook, a.k.a. tyee—a native term of honor that means "chief." I only hoped this beauty didn't twist the leader around our rudder.

No, the king was back, and I was still in business. I snapped the leader onto the wire in the gear tray and reached with my right hand for my gaff. I took the hundred-pound-test in my gloved hands and began to pull hand over hand. For traction, I pressed the monofilament tight against the wooden shaft of the gaff with my right hand as my left drew in more and more leader.

Suddenly the big fish broke the surface again, thrashing up a frenzy of white water and whipping its head back and forth. It failed to shake the hook.

Just don't give him any slack, I thought.

I braced and pulled with my back as well as my arms. This was one powerful fish! I drew the chinook in close, almost close enough to club, and then I remembered. *First fish goes back into the sea.* It was a Daniels family tradition to shake the first one loose.

But this is a fifty-pound king, I told myself as I gripped the end of the flasher that was toward the fish. Bent over the back of the boat, I made ready with the gaff poised high in the air. Then I froze.

I looked in the highliner's direction. He had just landed another and was looking at me with a big question mark above his head. His eyes were asking, *What in the world are you waiting for?*

Do it, I told myself, and I came down hard with the gaff, clubbing the big king squarely on the top of the head. With no further hesitation, I spun the gaff in my right hand and swung with a shorter swing, this time sinking the gaff hook deep through the cheek plate at the side of its head. Both hands on the gaff, I threw my body weight back, the big tyee filling up the sky as I swung it over my right shoulder and into the cleaning bin.

The clouds that had seemed so threatening had all sped by. The golden morning light fell on the gasping fish, for the time being lying still. In its first half minute out of the ocean, a king salmon's iridescence distills all the beauty of the earth and the stars. That's what my mother says, and she's an artist. My own eyes tell me she has it right. Beneath its dark sea green back, there's a swath of red-violet, then a brilliant band of metallic copper-gold. In the lower half of the fish, each silver scale sparkles like a diamond prism, refracting light into every color of the rainbow.

As the king's life drains away so does its color, and its magic, until all you have left is a dying fish thrashing in the bin, smearing itself in blood and slime and spattering you with the same.

At that moment, I had no time to dwell on the tragedy of every salmon pulled from the sea. From way back to my toddler days on the family boat, I was used to the slaughter. When the bite is on, you don't stop to think. You jerk the lure from the fish's mouth with the gaff hook and you slap the flasher on the rail, letting its lure swing free over the back of the boat. Then you reach for the gurdy lever as fast as you can to bring up the next spread.

A glance over the stern, and I saw that I had a king on the next one, and the next one. This was fishing. It was the first hour of the season—this school had never seen the gear before and they were going crazy over it.

Torsen was in constant motion on his side of the cockpit, whacking kings and hauling them aboard. "Yes sir!" I shouted.

I pulled three more kings from my tip line, then began snapping the spreads back onto the line and sending it back down. As soon as I had run it down thirty-two fathoms, I started in on the heavy and pulled two kings from it for a total of six, then returned its eleven lures to duty. Meanwhile, my tip line had been rattling for several minutes. It was time to pull it up again. It produced two cohos—silver salmon—and three more kings, including two over thirty pounds. I had only dreamed it could be like this.

By the time I pulled my heavy again, the salmon on its spreads had been hooked long enough to attract some bad company. One of the three I brought up had fresh wounds, two rows of tooth marks about four inches apart. "Shark," Tor said. "That fish won't sell; we'll call it dinner."

Our bins were close to full, and the bite was finally slowing. The skipper had me start cleaning while he worked all four lines. I reached for the next fish and the next, and the next. Don't cut your finger, I reminded myself. A rubber glove is no protection against a razor-sharp cleaning knife. I switched to cleaning the fish in the opposite bin whenever the captain came over to pull fish on my side. I kept the gaff for each side hosed clean of slippery slime and lying in the bottom of the cleaning cradle exactly where he would expect it at the moment he reached for it—one signal among many to show him he hadn't hired a greenhorn.

Tor made a slow U-turn to head back over the school. We headed north, in the direction we had come, with a couple hundred yards separating us from the line of trollers still heading south.

In a few minutes we were over the salmon again, and Tor was landing fish steady as before. The trollers were making the turn where the highliner had, falling in behind us. I cleaned fish as fast as I was able. One by one I sprayed them clean with salt water from the deck hose, then heaved them forward into the big white rinse tubs.

From blood vessels finer than the eye can see, the salmon gradually turn the rinse water bright red. Tor wanted them rinsing no longer than fifteen minutes. Otherwise they'd start to drop scales, and the man at the fish plant would call them number twos and pay us much less per pound.

Fifteen minutes by my watch, and I climbed out of the cockpit, slid the heavy lid of the fish hold a couple feet back, and dropped the rinsed fish onto the chipped ice on the floor of the hold below. I tried to drop the heavy ones as gently as I could. Keeping separate count of kings and cohos, I raced into the wheelhouse and marked the numbers in Tor's notebook. We were catching three kings for every coho, which is what you want: they're not only bigger, they pay three times as much per pound.

Back out on the deck, I spilled the bloody water from the rinse tubs, but no faster than the scupper slots could drain the mess back into the ocean—otherwise, it would have spilled all over the deck.

Leaning over the side with the pickle barrel, I scooped up three gallons or so of seawater at a time, careful not to let it get so full that it would break my back or pull me into the ocean. The bulwark was less than knee-high. I had to watch the swells or I would lose my balance.

"Do that from your knees," Tor barked. "I don't want you going overboard."

"Me neither," I said, and kept working. I thought I might have been due for a compliment, and his warning stung. Still, I should have known better. At least he seemed concerned about my safety.

The rinse bin on each side refreshed, I climbed down into the fish hold and began the stoop work I was hired for. I was set to begin stowing our treasure. Troll-caught are the finest restaurant-quality wild salmon, the most expensive on account of being the most labor intensive—cleaned and bled within minutes of being caught, iced a few degrees above freezing, then rushed to market by jet.

I began by bedding the forward right section of the hold with a few inches of ice. Then I returned to the central floor where I'd thrown the salmon. I lifted that fifty-pounder with both arms, duck-walked it forward, used the aluminum scoop to fill its body and gill cavity with ice, then laid it gently off to the right. Extra-large were paying $1.21 a pound. I was looking at a sixty-dollar fish. My share . . . nine dollars. Not bad!

One fish at a time, I repeated the process. I laid them out neatly and bedded them with ice when I was ready to start a new layer. I slid one of the cedar bin boards into position to contain the fish in that compartment.

My back was already fit to breaking. Hours of bending over the stern to gaff the fish, bending over the cleaning bin, and stooping in the hold were taking their toll. It felt like a fish knife was planted deep between my shoulder blades.

Last fish stowed, I returned to the central floor of the hold but stood up too soon. My skull met the framing under the plywood tray that supported our refrigerated groceries. I saw stars, and had a grim laugh at myself. Focus, Robbie!

I hoisted myself out of the fish hold onto the deck. Sliding the heavy cover back over the hatch, then blinking in the bright light, teeth clenched against the pain still ripping through my skull, I straightened my back and flexed my numb fingers. The chipped ice had a way of sliding inside the rubber gloves.

The wind had picked up and the *Petrel* was rolling in the slop. I nearly got pitched off balance, then braced just in time. Torsen was looking at me like I was a greenhorn.

"Take your side again," the captain hollered. "We gotta bring 'em in faster. The sea lions are onto us."

I looked to our wake but couldn't see any sea lions. As I swung into the cockpit and started to pull the port tip line, the skipper reached for the hayrack and pulled himself out of the cockpit. He braced his way across the rolling deck and disappeared into the wheelhouse. This was my chance to look around more carefully, with Tor away, to see if I could find where his mysterious metal plaque had gotten off to.

No luck. It wasn't anywhere to be found. I looked up as the captain appeared at the wheelhouse door. He had a pocket lighter in one hand and what looked like a small stick of dynamite in the other. His face was contorted into a hard angry knot. Muttering darkly, he lit the bomb and tossed it over the side. A second after hitting the water, it exploded. At the back of our wake, two startled sea lions leaped halfway out of the water.

Our raiders with the big bearlike heads were Steller's sea lions. Some of the bulls are bigger than the biggest bears in Alaska.

For the time being, they let us be. Maybe they dropped back to pursue a free lunch from the boat behind us on the drag.

The captain stayed sour even though we were catching salmon hand over fist. If his mood was the result of his back aching, I wished he would take some more Tylenol. His disposition was giving me some pains of my own, so I tried to cheer him up. "I never dreamed it could be like this!" I yelled after landing yet another one as long as my arm. Its head was three times the size of my fist.

Torsen looked startled, almost like he'd forgotten I was there. "It seldom is," he replied, his weathered face slowly breaking into a smile as he watched me work my lines. "Doesn't get any better than this."

The bite finally tailed off in the early afternoon. The tide had ebbed, Tor explained, pulling the feed farther out to sea and the predator kings with it. We cleaned fish until one-thirty. "What do you say we fix some eggs," he said finally.

After nine hours of work, it was time for breakfast.

"What's the count?" Tor grunted from the galley as he washed his hands in the sink.

"A hundred and three kings, thirty-seven cohos."

"That's not half bad," he said with a grin. "Not bad for a morning's work."

7

AFTER OUR AFTERNOON BREAKFAST, the fish quit biting in Veta Bay. We pulled our gear and the skipper headed south until we joined another small fleet of trollers off of Granite Point. We were soon working the drag between Granite and Cape Chirikof.

The action picked up again, and I landed and cleaned king salmon well into the evening. We were the last of the trollers to steer for Cape Chirikof's polished limestone slopes. Motoring past a deep sea cave, we slipped inside a finger of water behind the bony tip of the cape and dropped anchor in the company of half a dozen other trollers. There was wind in the forecast;

the rest of the boats had run for a more protected spot around the lee side of the island. "What do you say we fix something to eat?" Tor said.

While the salmon was baking, I gave the skipper's library a good looking over. It was above his bunk and spanned its length—three spill-proof shelves full. Most of the books were about Alaska and Canada. Some were about trolling, going back to the earliest days of hand trolling from small skiffs. There were quite a few about the Russians in Alaska. I was paging through one of them when I spotted something familiar—a picture of a plaque a lot like the one I had seen on the boat. This one didn't have a number, or the Russian writing, but it had a two-headed eagle. The caption said the photo was of a metal crest that was a gift from the Russians to the Tlingits.

Then it hit me.

Not only had Tor found me trespassing on his boat, he'd caught me looking at what must have been a valuable treasure. Maybe he'd taken me for a thief—maybe a thief looking for something very specific. I flipped the book around so he could see it from where he was working at the stove. "Look what I found," I said.

Tor's face hardened, but that was nothing new. I kept going. "It's like yours, right? I saw something like this myself once, but it was on a totem pole. That's pretty cool, that the Russians got the double-headed eagle from the Indians."

Tor stared at me like I was dumb as a ling cod. "You got that backward. The Indians got it from the Russians."

"Oh," I said.

That was it. Tor didn't say another word about the plaque. He just brought a platter of salmon to the table with some rice and sat down across from me. I avoided his eyes at first, wondering what new trouble I'd gotten myself into, but he seemed content to change the subject. "Are you sore from working down in the hold?" he asked.

I was more than a little relieved. "I can barely lift my fork," I answered. "A hundred and forty-one kings, Tor. I can barely believe it. I suppose you've caught more than that in a day?"

"Close to three hundred once."

"By yourself? How?"

"Just did it."

"Over the years, how many kings make what you would call a good day?"

"I'm always trying to break fifty. Fifty is a good day."

"And we caught a hundred and forty!"

"Sure, but the price is down, remember? These days you have to catch a hundred to make what you used to make catching fifty. So in reality, we caught seventy."

"I guess it must be pretty discouraging."

"I plead guilty to being cynical about our industry.

If you'd been fishing as many years as I have, you would be, too."

"I'm trying to work my numbers," I explained. "Not on the cohos; I know they're only paying thirty cents a pound. Any guesses what the average weight of our king salmon is running?"

"Close to seventeen pounds, dressed out."

"What are they going to pay if we factor in number ones, number twos, and extra large?"

"On average, around ninety cents a pound."

I reached for a pencil as he was serving the salmon. The fish was moist as can be, just the way I like it. Torsen had baked it in a mustard sauce and put slices of red onion on top. "Let's see," I said, "that's about twenty-three hundred and eighty pounds of king salmon down in the hold, times ninety cents, would bring two thousand one hundred and forty-two dollars. Fifteen percent is my share, which would be . . . three hundred and twenty-one dollars. Can that be right?"

Torsen went back to eating and looked at me impatiently. "Sure, that's right. Give yourself another ten or twenty bucks for the cohos."

"That's amazing! I'm already out of the red and into the black!"

"Eat up," he said.

"Man, I can't believe it! I picked the right boat, eh?"

"The other boats might be doing better."

"No way—I've been watching. Say, how come you

don't play the radio out the deck speakers so you can hear what the other boats are saying about the bite?"

"Too distracting. It's just talk, anyway. Guys complain they aren't catching fish when you know full well they are, and vice versa. If they talk about gear that's working, it might be to throw you off. The only time they tell the truth is among their own code group, and then it's not on the regular frequency; it's on their second radio that's scrambled so nobody but them can pick it up. I tune into the weather when I'm in the wheelhouse. I pay attention to news about when the season might close. What else do I really need to know?"

"This salmon is as good as my mom's," I said, "and that's saying something. She'd serve it with kelp pickles and beach asparagus, though."

"Never had 'em."

"You don't know what you're missing!"

"Prince of Wales Island has been pretty well logged off, hasn't it?"

"Pretty much," I said. "The logging communities went bust. Most of those folks left."

"And the commercial fishing is going bust on account of all the farmed salmon flooding the market. Prince of Wales must be hurting."

"It is," I said. "There's government jobs, that sort of thing, sport fishing lodges . . . and there's always subsistence. The subsistence families will be able to hang on."

The big man looked irritated. "Is that what your

parents want for you? Just to hang on living a subsistence life?"

"Not really," I said, surprised by his reaction. "My sister thinks that's what she wants, but she's ten and doesn't really know. My parents figure that I'll probably find my way off the island, but I'm not so sure. I love Prince of Wales, and I'd hate to give up the fishing."

"There's no future in it."

"Well, it would just be a sideline, that's what I'm thinking. If I had a regular job the other nine months, like teaching for example, then the fishing wouldn't be do or die."

"Like that teacher from Craig does."

"Exactly. Teaching might be the way to go. I get excited about learning stuff, and I like kids. Who knows, I might end up working with Julie."

"I don't suppose your parents can send you to college."

"No, but I could maybe get some scholarships and loans, and partly work my way through. I used to think I would come home from college in the summers and make big money as a deckhand. Maybe the prices will come back up."

"Don't count on it."

Enthusiastic, the man wasn't. "Hey, Tor," I said, "you've hardly told me anything about yourself."

"Not much to tell. I catch fish, eat, sleep."

"I was just wondering about where you grew up, your family, that kind of stuff."

"Now you're snooping again. Another time, maybe. It's after ten. When I'm fishing, I'm in bed by nine-thirty."

"I was just curious, that's all."

"I don't pay you for your curiosity," he growled, and lay down on his bunk. He was snoring before I'd even cleared the dishes. It was unbelievable, the man's talent for falling asleep.

I scrubbed dishes to the tune of his snoring. It was hard to stand at the sink. That knife I imagined in my back seemed to have its tip in my spinal cord. Thinking about the plaque distracted me some, and I kept trying to get a handle on my moody captain. One minute he could be laughing and hauling in kings, the next he was so gloomy it scared me.

When the last dish was done, it was all I could do to climb down the ladder to my bunk.

8

ON FOUR AND A HALF HOURS of sleep, I was fishing again. We were the first to pull out of the hidey-hole behind Cape Chirikof, the first to drop our gear. Early on we caught a few kings, but then the bite went dead. The wind was out of the west, pushing bigger seas than I'd ever been on. When a troller opposite us was down in the trough of a swell, all you could see was its mast and the tops of its poles. Welcome to the Gulf of Alaska, Robbie.

I asked the captain if the big seas had anything to do with the kings making themselves scarce. Tor scowled. "The kings run deep. What's going on at the surface has nothing to do with it."

Then he squinted, seeming to stare at my hands.

"What's that on your glove?" he demanded.

On the thumb and forefinger of my right hand, there were smudges of black grease. "No wonder we aren't catching anything," he said.

"Must be from the gurdy bushings," I muttered. I didn't know why he was so upset. "I'll have to watch it closer."

"Get out of the way," was all he said as he crowded into my corner of the cockpit. I had to squeeze past him and stand by helplessly as he began to pull my lines.

I still hadn't figured out why he was pulling them—I didn't have a fish on—but I found out soon enough. He found a spot of grease on each of the lines.

Tor wasn't going to cut me any slack on this. He wouldn't even look at me as he replaced the hootchies and cleaned the greasy spots off the steel fishing line. Then came the lecture. "Salmon can smell grease a mile off," he said, his sharp eyes drilling into mine. "Keep in mind, kid, they can smell their way back to the exact stretch of whatever little creek they were hatched at, no matter that it's a thousand miles from the ocean."

It was pointless to make excuses, although fatigue would have been the first on my list. Sorry, I was about to say, but I knew *sorry* wouldn't cut it. "I'll watch it closer," I said. "I won't let this happen again."

"Go get a new glove," he ordered, not that I wouldn't have anyway.

A while later we had a small flurry of kings, three

on my side, two on his. After I'd cleaned mine, he came over to my side, pointed to one just as I was about to throw it forward into the rinse bin, and said, "That one legal?"

He'd shown me how he'd built the cleaning cradles exactly twenty-eight inches long, which was the legal minimum for kings. I had forgotten to check. With the skipper watching close, I flopped the fish back into the cradle, hoping he was wrong. He wasn't; it fell short by an inch.

"Set that one aside down below," he said, "so they don't catch us trying to sell it. See if you can keep your mind on what you're doing. Quit that daydreamin' and do what I'm paying you to do."

I'd been working like a mule ever since I got on his boat. I couldn't believe he was accusing me of slacking off.

A dark cloud over my head, I went below to ice the few fish we'd caught. When I got back up top, Tor was landing salmon and the pole on my side was rattling, too. I moved across the deck as low as a crab, bracing all the way against the heavy rolling of the boat. Torsen had his eyes on me like I was a greenhorn about to take a swim. I dropped into the cockpit and started bringing up my tip line. I could feel his eyes on the back of my head. I tried to work faster than I should have. As I was hauling in a big king hand over hand, the boat pitched in the direction of the fish. All it takes is an instant of slack in the leader. Just that fast, the fish shook the hook and was gone. I looked in Tor's direction. Naturally, he was watching.

My whole life, I'd never felt time go so slow. This one morning was like a life sentence.

It got worse. I'd never fished in that much wind. It blew the leaders around and made it tough to keep them from tangling with each other as I arranged them along the rail. At one point I thought I'd snapped a leader onto the wire in the gear tray but I'd missed. As soon as I let go, the entire spread, flasher and hootchie and all, plummeted to the bottom of the Pacific Ocean.

My highliner watched it go. He looked at me with undisguised contempt. He didn't say a thing, just reached for one of his spare spreads and handed it to me.

Midday, we made sandwiches from cold cuts. Lunch took fifteen minutes and felt like fifteen hours. If Tor wanted to make me feel like a herring in the talons of an eagle, he was succeeding.

After we ate, we pulled the gear and ran north to Noyes Island and the Cape Addington Grounds. The wind quit and it turned flat calm. The sport boats appeared from the fishing lodges. The sun came out and you could see halfway to China. The bite picked up. Suddenly we had a couple dozen kings, and I quit moping. Just as suddenly, the action was over. Back and forth we worked the drag between the rocky foot of Addington to the big haystack rock to the north. Late in the afternoon the sport boats sped off, and the trollers had the evening light to themselves.

In all my life I had never seen such a spectacular

sight as Cape Addington. I knew my mom would have loved to paint it. Trees with wind-tortured shapes clung to the crevices at the very top of the gray cliffs. Eons of winter gales had scoured the stone clean and so smooth you wished you could touch it. Along the tide line, the grays gave way to reds and oranges. To the south and east, the trees reached all the way to the base of a long arm curling off the cape. It was mostly composed of huge limestone blocks cut so squarely they might have fallen from an Incan wall.

My boss noticed I was admiring the view. "No finer cape in Alaska," he grunted, "unless it's Edgecumbe, north of Sitka. Addington and Edgecumbe were both named by Captain Cook. Did you know that?"

"I didn't," I admitted.

"Seems like somebody who might be a teacher in southeast Alaska would at least be interested in the history."

"I am," I protested. I thought of that Russian plaque of his. I was way interested in that piece of history.

We managed to boat a few more fish. Just as I flopped a big king into the bin, I looked up and there was the *Julie Kristine* right across from us. And there she was, Julie Kristine herself, waving just like she'd said she would, then pumping her fist up and down to show she was excited about me landing fish. Her son, Bear, was doing the same. Her father, as big a man as Torsen, was a blur of motion on the far side of the cockpit, gaffing a king.

I waved back, and hollered so loud they might have even heard me.

Tor just stared as he popped his pain pills and washed them down.

I missed being on a family boat. No question, they were having a lot more fun.

Eight P.M. and the *Storm Petrel* was still on the drag, even though the fishing had gone completely dead. I sat at the wheelhouse table looking over the bow, and Torsen sat in his captain's chair behind the wheel, staring straight ahead. I could pretty well guess what he was thinking. His back hadn't seized up on him, and if it wasn't going to, hiring me had been a mistake. I was like a weed in a perfect garden, just an annoyance. Every time he turned around, I was right there.

The *Storm Petrel* was a bigger boat than my family's, but it sure felt smaller. And this was only our second day.

Tor studied a pink booklet, the tide tables, while glancing occasionally to the bow. From inside the wheelhouse of a troller, the fishing is easily monitored even though you can't see the trolling poles. There are ropes rigged from the poles down to bungee cords that connect to the bow with little bells attached. When you've got fish on, the bungees jump and the bells ring.

These tattletales, as they're called, had nothing more to tell that day. Dusk found us anchoring in Steamboat Bay, around the north point of Noyes Island. Torsen, back on his regular schedule, was asleep by nine-thirty. I stayed up only a few minutes longer to tabulate my earnings for the day, about seventy-five dollars.

On our third day the early bite off of Addington was promising, with Tor landing fish in a dense fog. I felt vindicated: he wouldn't have been able to fish at all without a deckhand in the wheelhouse to watch the radar monitor. I also did the steering, from the captain's chair, avoiding phantom boats that were close but invisible.

The fog lifted late morning. With the tide out, the fishing was worse than poor. Tor was back in his captain's chair, rubbing his beard and staring over the bow. Something about his expression reminded me of an Irish lord, a spiny rockfish that scares off predators with its looks.

I killed the downtime reading one of his Alaska books.

If I could have charted Tor's moods, it would have been one crazy graph. Over lunch, to my surprise, he started talking about himself and his family. He was born in Bella Coola, British Columbia, a fishing community founded by Norwegian immigrants. "It looks exactly like a fjord in Norway," Tor said fondly. "Huge cliffs and hanging waterfalls above the valley floor. Better than Norway on account of the gigantic red cedars."

Tor still had two sisters living there, and a third who had moved to Florida. "Were you ever married?" I asked.

"Yes," he said slowly. "Her name was Marie. Her folks had moved up to Bella Coola from Washington State when she was a couple years out of high school. Bought the town's only general store. I used to hang around the store so I could talk to her. Marie was different from the other girls I'd grown up with. She wanted to be out on the water every chance she got. A born sailor, she was, and she loved the work."

"She liked to fish?"

"That goes without saying. We got married and trolled together for five years out of Bella Coola."

"Did you have any kids?"

"We had a daughter, Grace. She loved going out on the boat with us. When Grace got a little older, closer to school age, Marie decided that we ought to move down to Washington. Grace would have cousins to play with. Marie's sister lived down there, in Anacortes. So that's what we did."

"Did you quit trolling then?"

"No, I kept trolling out of Anacortes, sometimes down the Oregon coast as far as San Francisco, but mostly up to Alaska. Alaska has always been my favorite."

I wasn't sure I should ask my next question. He'd been talking about his wife like she was in the past. "Are you still with Marie?"

"Lost her," he said, and looked away.

I didn't know what that meant. I didn't know what to say. "What about Grace?" I asked.

"She lives in Port Townsend. That's less than an

hour from Port Angeles, where I live. She's been wanting me to move closer to her, even though we don't get along all that great. She's always nagging me to get something done about my back. She's a nurse, so she's inclined to think cutting on it will fix everything. I'm not so sure."

"It's good to have people worrying about you, I suppose. Shows they care."

"I guess, but I'm not as stove up as she thinks." Torsen got up, fixed us both mugs of coffee, then sat back down. "Biggest problem with Grace is, she lost her mother on account of me."

I was in over my head. I held my hot coffee mug in both hands and stared into it.

When I didn't say anything, the old-timer, looking straight ahead over the bow, said, "Grace was in the wheelhouse with me, twelve years old, when I lost her mother off the back of the boat."

"Tor, I'm—"

"It was off the Oregon coast. Rough water, but rough water was nothing new to her. Marie liked to work the back of the boat. Grace and I were in the wheelhouse and I had the radio going. Maybe if I hadn't been listening to the fishermen chatter on the VHF, I would have heard Marie yell out. I never heard a thing. There were other boats in the area. . . . I made my best guess where we'd been when she went over. All the fishing boats searched, the Coast Guard searched. . . . We never found her. Sometimes that happens, the sea just doesn't give a body up."

I was so stunned I couldn't speak. I don't know why, but I was picturing the bright orange tentacles of the octopus that almost pulled me into the ocean when I was three. I can't imagine what it would be like to lose one of my family off the *Chimes*. I just know I would never be the same.

"I'm sorry," was all I could say.

To my huge relief, the tattletales started jumping and ringing. We were back to fishing. We had a decent evening bite, and so did the sea lions.

Right when the bite was going good, one of those huge Steller's lions popped up in our wake with one of our kings in its jaws, shaking that big fish like it was a rag doll. The sea lions eat all but the salmon's head, cleverly avoiding the hook. The leader usually breaks close to the trolling wire; you lose the entire spread.

"I'll take care of this one," I told Tor, climbing out of the cockpit before he could. In the wheelhouse, I didn't see Tor's lighter next to the little pile of bombs he kept ready at the table. I reached for a box of barn-burner matches instead.

I had to be quick, and I knew I'd never be able to light the match out on the deck. The wind had come up. I lit the match right there at the table.

The boat pitched just as I was reaching with my free hand for one of the bombs. I dropped my match and it fell to the table—a hair away from the tips of two of the fuses.

Tor had already told me about a guy who lost his hand to one of these things. They were called bombs for a reason. I slammed my hand down on the table, knocking the match to the floor. I looked in the direction it went, and there was Tor filling up the doorway.

"You fool kid!" he thundered. "You could have blown up the wheelhouse and sunk my boat!"

9

HAD A BAD NIGHT. I couldn't shake the image of the captain, furious at me, yelling angry words, then storming off into a cold silence. In my dreams he was towering over me, threatening to shove me into the freezing waves.

I woke to drizzle across the face of Steamboat Bay. A long, raw day of fishing was in store. So far we'd been working dry, getting away with murder. Now it was back to normal in rainy Southeast.

My mind's weather was just as gloomy. Tor didn't want me aboard and I didn't want to be there. I'd be doing us both a favor if I called this off.

When Tor, over donuts, started talking about selling the fish we had, then heading north for the grounds off of Coronation Island and the west coast of Baranof Island, I went with my gut. "I'm thinking I'll get off at Craig, when you go in to sell," I announced.

I was surprised by how stunned he looked, like a fish hit with a gaff club. "Get off? I thought you signed on for king season."

"I did. But I'm thinking about changing my mind."

"Bad weather, is that it? Rainy day blues?"

"I'm used to working in rain—we get ten or twelve feet a year in Protection. I kind of miss my family, I guess. The fishing doesn't look like it's going to be that great, and—"

"Hold on there. Four days, and you want to go home? Homesick, are you? You miss your mother, I bet."

"And my sister and my father," I said, trying to ignore his sarcasm.

"Fishing doesn't look like it's going to be that great? How can you tell? We've only gotten started."

"They might close the season in a few days."

"Or they might not. We've listened every evening. There's no talk of that."

"Well, there's another reason."

"And what's that?"

"I've been making too many mistakes."

"What are you talking about?"

I named them for him, from the grease on my glove to the sea lion bombs.

"That's all you can come up with?" he growled.

"Isn't that enough? I almost blew up the boat last night!"

"Well, you didn't, and you won't make that mistake twice. You've been a big help to me."

"You never said so. . . ."

The highliner seemed genuinely astonished. "What do you want from me? You're sixteen years old. You need me to pat you on the head and tell you you've been a good boy? Is that what you want?"

"No, no, I—"

"I think I know what this is really about. You're thinking you won't make any money, am I right? To start saving for college or whatever?"

"It wasn't realistic. Julie warned me."

"What does she know? You could make real good money, on this boat, this king season, if you weren't a quitter. Is that what you are, a quitter?"

"Not really."

"I'm not even going to give you the chance to quit. I'm holding you to king season, like you signed on for. Forget about getting off in Craig. I'm not going to sell in Craig."

It was my turn to be surprised. "Where will you sell?"

"I'm not going in. This first round, I'll sell offshore, to a tender. The *Angie* is anchored in Kelly Cove, around the back of Noyes Island."

This news hit me hard. I couldn't get off his boat even if I wanted to. I felt seasick—I never get seasick. "You really think the fishing's going to pick up?"

"Look, whether it does or not, you can still make some money."

Tor seemed determined to keep me on the boat. "I give up," I said. "I'm totally baffled. I don't know what you're talking about."

"Your time has come."

"My time for what?"

"To learn about that Russian plaque you're so interested in."

Tor got up and went over to his bunk. From under the foot of his mattress, he pulled out the metal plate. He set it on the table and pushed it in my direction.

"You'll appreciate this, being as you're part Russian. Go ahead, feel it, touch it. Looks old, doesn't it?"

"It does."

"Well, it is. You're looking at only the third possession plaque ever discovered. It's the real deal."

"Possession plaque? What's that mean?"

"See this writing down here? In Russian it says, 'This land belongs to Russia.' You ever been in the Bishop's House Museum, the old Russian Bishop's House in Sitka?" His eyes were gleaming.

"I went there once. I've been in the Russian cathedral, too."

"Forget about the cathedral. The Bishop's House has a copy on display—behind Plexiglas—of Possession Plaque Number 12. The original is locked up in a safe somewhere. It's too valuable to be shown to the public, especially since it was the only one ever found."

"Until this one?"

"No, until Number 15."

"Who found Number 15?"

"I did."

"How about this one—Number 13?"

"I did. Both have the double-headed eagle crest, which makes them even more valuable. Number 12, the one in Sitka, doesn't have it. They weren't all made exactly the same."

"Your two—how did you find them?"

"It wasn't easy," the highliner said evasively. He appeared to be in uncharted waters.

Now that he'd told me this much, I was dying to know more. "I mean, where did you find them?"

"You don't need to know that," he snapped, like a dog over its food dish.

"Okay," I said. "How about the one they have in Sitka? Where was that one found?"

"About six miles north of town. They dug it up back in 1935 at the original site of Russian Sitka."

"The fort the Tlingits demolished?"

"So you know a little history after all. That's right—St. Michael's Redoubt. The fort was built in 1799, and the Tlingits weren't too happy about it. Your native ancestors had been fighting tooth and nail to keep the white men—the Americans, the British, the Russians—from getting a toehold on their lands. They were happy to swap furs for guns and knives and cookware, but then they just wanted the intruders to go back to wherever they'd come from. It was the

Russians they were especially afraid of. The Russians had been enslaving the people from the Aleutian Islands to hunt sea otters for them ever since Bering's discovery of Alaska back in 1741. The elite in China were paying more for a single sea otter pelt than a working man could make in a year."

"I never understood how so few Russians could enslave so many hundreds of hunters."

"Easy. 'Follow our gunship in your kayaks or we kill all the women and children back in the village.'"

"Okay, I got it. They had cannons."

"By 1799, the sea otters were all but extinct in the Aleutians, and pretty well wiped out around Kodiak and southcentral Alaska. The Russians moved on to where there were plenty. They got a toehold in the islands of southeast Alaska, the homeland of the Tlingits."

"Who fought back."

"With a vengeance. Alexander Baranof, the head of the Russian-American Company, was away when the Tlingits stormed the fort in 1802. They leveled it. But in 1804, Baranof returned with a bigger and better gunship and hundreds of his Aleut slaves. The Tlingits fought hard, until one night they retreated. Baranof built his new fort on the best high ground available—the Tlingits' former village—and ringed it with cannons. The Tlingits were never enslaved, but they did come around to trading with Baranof. They'd already been trading with the Americans—the 'Boston men'—

for more than a decade."

"What's this all about? Where do the possession plaques fit in?"

Torsen looked at me long and hard, as if trying to make up his mind about me. If he didn't trust me, why was he telling me all this?

"You made this your business," he said with a cold stare, "snooping around on my boat like you did."

A chill went down my spine. "I thought we could forget that."

"History and eggs, neither can be unscrambled. Just listen. You're involved, we can't change that. Maybe it will come out to your benefit. In the Bishop's House, they'll tell you there were twenty plaques all together. There are records of how many, but not where they were planted."

"Planted?"

"That's right, buried in the ground. Each had its number engraved on it, along with the words 'This land belongs to Russia.' They knew about the Spanish exploring up here not so long after Bering's discovery, and they knew about Captain Cook's search for the Northwest Passage in 1778. They knew that another English captain, Vancouver, had charted all these islands and waters in the early 1790s."

"Vancouver named Port Protection," I said. "He ducked in there to ride out a storm."

Tor nodded gruffly at my interruption, then plowed ahead. "The Russians were eager to take possession of as much of the sea otter habitat as they could before the U.S., England, or Spain did. They made twenty of these plaques, and planted them along the northwest coast, in order to stake their claim."

"If the plaques were buried, how would the other countries know that the land had been claimed?"

Torsen laughed. "You have to get into their mindset. Spain and some of the other colonial powers had been doing the same thing for centuries. Theoretically, it was so they could trump some Johnny-come-lately. Let's say a ship's captain was about to claim the area for his own country. They could dig up the plaque for him and say, 'Look here, fellow, we've been here since way back.'"

"But there's no date on this thing."

"My guess is, the Russians left that out on purpose."

"Because the plaques were made after the Spanish, the English, and the Americans were already in the area?"

"That's what I'm thinking."

"You found Number 13 and Number 15. How?

With a sly smile, he said, "An antique dealer I know put me on to them. He has a warehouse in Port Angeles. It's small, but he moves a lot of stuff through it. He hits every garage sale and antique auction within a hundred miles. A couple of years back, in Port Townsend, he came by an old sea chest with the imperial eagle of czarist Russia on its clasp."

"I'll bet that was valuable."

Torsen shrugged. "Not like you might think. It had

to be restored; some fool had kept it in a leaky wood-shed. On account of the rusty Russian eagle, it was appraised at three hundred dollars. The owner wanted four hundred. The antique dealer bought it for three fifty. By the time he got it home, he was thinking it was heavier than it appeared, and he was wondering why that was."

"Two of the plaques were hidden inside?"

"No, but something else was, in a false bottom."

Timing being everything to a fisherman, Torsen paused, then set the hook. "The trunk's false bottom concealed a journal, a very old journal from Russian America. A journal that records where the plaques were hidden."

I couldn't believe it. "This is amazing. And now you've got the journal?"

"I've got the journal," Tor said gravely.

"You must have had to pay through the nose for it."

"Not at all," Tor said with a grin. "You see, I'm that antique dealer. That's what I do with my winters down in Port Angeles. I sold Number 15 already."

"For how much?"

Torsen laughed. "More money than you've ever seen, but less than this one'll bring, and the next one."

"The next one?"

"That's where you come in, Robbie. In addition to the fishing, of course. Are you up for a little adventure? These plaques aren't so easy to locate, and you could help, especially if my back goes out on me. I found this

Number 13 a couple of weeks ago. Number 15, I found that last year. Now listen carefully. If we find another one, I'll double whatever you make fishing. That's why you don't want to quit me and go home to your mother."

There was more going on here than I could figure out. I held back, despite the pull of the plaque and the money.

Torsen took offense. "Well?" he demanded. "What kind of fool are you? Aren't you trying to make as much money as you can?"

"That's a lot to think about, all right," I managed. I was wondering if all this was legal.

"Is this a finders-keepers situation?" I asked as carefully as possible. "I mean, the plaques are yours to sell?"

"Treasure law," Torsen said without hesitating. "Like finding gold from the wreck of a Spanish galleon."

Doubling my fishing money, that was a phenomenal offer, especially if we could catch a lot of fish. Tor was going to head north and try new water. The man was used to filling his hold. Here was my chance to make some real money. I had to keep my eye on the ball.

"I'm game," I announced, with a smile thrown in for good measure.

"That's better," Torsen said. "You make us some eggs and Alpo, I'll steer for Kelly Cove. As soon as we sell, we're on our way."

"Alpo?"

"Spam, Robbie. Sliced and fried. Grab three of those big potatoes and make us some home fries. Fry everything in that bacon grease we saved from yesterday. You can cook, can't you? Open a jar of salsa. Slice and butter some bagels, warm 'em, don't petrify 'em. We'll split a cantaloupe, and don't forget the orange juice and coffee."

"You're on," I said.

This was going to be something new. Breakfast at breakfast time.

We ate, and soon after that we cranked up the trolling poles. At nine knots, it wasn't long until I was throwing the fenders over the side, and we were snubbing up to the *Angie*, a boat twice our size. I scrambled into the hold and Tor waved the big fish bucket down. I dug the salmon out by hand and laid them one by one in the wide bucket.

The last fish off-loaded, we motored off so I could muck out the old ice. Then we cozied up to the *Angie* again and they lowered the ice hose down to me. The guys on the *Angie* recognized Torsen from years back and were surprised he had a deckhand. They kidded him about getting soft. "Is he worth his salt?" I heard the fish buyer ask.

"The kid does it all," I heard Tor reply. "I'm just along for the ride."

10

B Y NOON WE WERE BACK on the outside water. Tor
steered north by northwest. On the way out to the
Pedro grounds off of St. Joseph Island, the north
wind picked up. Before long it was blowing twenty
knots and the *Storm Petrel* was plunging over foaming
crests and diving into the troughs. Big time, I thought.
Big-time water. I felt like I was on Captain Cook's ship,
or Vancouver's.

Visibility was poor on account of the rain and the
bow spray lashing the wheelhouse windows. "Are we
going to put the gear down?" I asked the captain.

"Why wouldn't we?" he barked.

"I just haven't fished in anything like this before."

"There's a first time for everything. Throw on

some warm clothes before you put on your rain gear."

There were only a couple of trollers in sight, and they were heading for cover. No whales were to be seen, and the *Storm Petrel* was the only bird in sight. It was just us, hobbyhorsing alone through wind and rain and heavy seas.

As I got dressed to go outside, I reminded myself that a man overboard in these freezing seas has no chance without a survival suit. Tor had the suits, but you can't work in one. They're too cumbersome. Stay focused, Robbie.

The fishing was tough. The wind tangled the leaders as I retrieved them; it was difficult for me to keep my feet. Heading north on the drag, we'd smack into the waves and get slowed down. Tor had to give it much more throttle than normal just to maintain trolling speed. Heading south, the following seas nearly broke into the cockpit. "How much wind can you still fish?" I shouted to Torsen over the weather.

"Twenty-five knots," he shouted back. "But it isn't much fun."

A couple hours later, and not a single fish, we pulled the gear. "I can't believe I'm out in weather this rough," I yelled.

Tor shook his head. "You ain't seen nothing yet."

Tor wanted to start working north and chew up some miles. After twenty miles of even rougher seas—the wind was blowing forty knots—we anchored in Aats Bay on the north end of Coronation Island. No other trollers kept us company. No wonder, after the open sea crossing we'd made to get there.

It kept blowing through the night. Twice, our anchor lost its grip on the bottom. Through layers of sleep, I was aware of the vibrations of the dragging anchor, but I didn't fully wake up when the engine came to life. It was the captain's responsibility to reposition and keep the boat off the rocks.

By morning the blow was all but over. We trolled back and forth across Windy Bay, the cleft in the island's cliffy windward shore, picking up only four cohos. "Coronation is either really good or really lousy," Tor said. "It's lousy today. Let's keep pushing north. If the fishing slows down, we'll hunt for treasure instead."

There was sea salt in his tangled beard and piracy in his voice. This Torsen seemed bigger than life, the reincarnation of some great seafarer. My mind drifted back to the plaques. "Finders keepers?" I wondered. Could that be? Or had I fallen in with a modern-day pirate?

With the snowcapped peaks of Baranof Island looming ever closer, we crossed Christian Sound. A dozen salmon trollers were working a drag at Baranof's southern tip, outside the tide rips swirling around Cape Ommaney. We joined them, but picked up only a few kings.

Tor didn't stay long to see if the fishing would improve. We pulled out and headed north along Baranof's rugged western coast. With little success, we fished off of Snipe Bay. We spent the night of July 6 inside the bay. Come daylight we fished farther north, off of Whale Bay, but all we caught were some accidental additions to our dinner menu—red snapper and halibut—when the lures on our lowest spreads passed too close to the top of an undersea hill.

Before we could escape to deeper water, the port pole was jerking like we'd hooked a whale. One of the cannonballs was dragging bottom; we could have lost major gear and time. Tor cursed a blue streak but had only himself to blame. He'd let too many minutes go by without checking the GPS monitor and the Fathometer.

That evening we ran past the mouth of Sitka Sound. Our bow was pointed northwest, toward the colossal volcano of Mount Edgecumbe, on the southern flank of Kruzof Island. Sunset found us sheltering in the lee of tiny St. Lazaria Island, where small dark birds by the tens of thousands—nesting storm petrels—were swarming the skies, making their last feeding runs before dark. Shortly after dawn we joined thirty or more trollers working the drag off Cape Edgecumbe's dark volcanic cliffs.

Tor had hit it big there in years past, but fifteen hours of fishing yielded a grand total of six kings. After anchoring in Gilmer Bay, along Kruzof's northern shore, Tor listened closely to the radio. There was still no talk of king season closing, which meant the quota for Southeast wasn't close to being met. There were still plenty of salmon out there that hadn't been caught. The talk among the fisherman had it that the action was picking up around Cape Addington, back where we'd started. Some of the trollers working the drag between Gilmer Bay and Cape Edgecumbe were going to speed south come first light.

"Not us," Tor said. "We keep working north."

"Are we getting closer to a plaque?"

"I've got a metallic taste in my mouth."

"Do you know what number it has on it?"

"It should be Number 11. It's the one they planted before the one at the original Sitka fort."

"Do you have the journal aboard?"

"Only the information I need. The journal itself is in a nice safe place."

"Whose was it?" I asked.

Torsen gave me a glance as sharp as the pirate's knife I was picturing in his teeth.

"I guess I don't really need to know," I said before he had the chance to.

"You got that right."

As we sat down to baked halibut a few minutes later, the storyteller in him won out. By now I was used to his ups and downs and should have expected it. "The man who kept the journal was named Rezanov," Tor said, a wide smile suddenly crossing his face. "Listen close, I'll tell you a story.

"Nikolai Rezanov was the man back in the capital—St. Petersburg—who was the driving force behind the Russian-America Company. He aimed to expand Russian America as far south as possible, to the Columbia River and even to the fringes of Spanish territory in San Francisco Bay."

"Didn't the Russians build a fort in northern California?"

"Fort Ross."

"Was that Rezanov's idea?"

"His idea, yes, but it came after his time, and never amounted to much without him. Who's telling this story, me or you?"

"You are, Captain."

"Then give me the chance," he said with a scowl that put me on notice not to call him Captain. "In the summer of 1803, Rezanov began a monumental ocean journey to the northern Pacific. He had two goals: to open Japan to Russian trade and to survey Russian America. The Russian-America Company was his baby, but he'd never laid eyes on Alaska.

"Two sailing frigates that he bought from the British took him around Europe, down the length of Africa, across the Indian Ocean and then the Pacific to Hawaii. That's where, in 1804, he learned about the Tlingit rebellion at Sitka, and that Baranof was regrouping at Kodiak. Rezanov dispatched one of his ships to Alaska to help Baranof fight the Tlingits, and headed for Japan to take care of his mission there.

"He arrived at Nagasaki with three hundred thousand rubles worth of gifts for the ruler, but the Japanese were a closed society and he had to wait six months just to get an interview with an official. Take a hike, was the answer he got. The Japanese didn't care spit for his gifts or for commerce with Russia.

"Rezanov left in a rage for Russian Siberia. From the Kamchatka Peninsula, he sailed on to the Aleutian Islands, where he found out that Russian America was more primitive than he had ever imagined. The good news was, they treated him like royalty. People ran in front of him laying boards on the ground so he wouldn't get his feet muddy.

"Rezanov sailed on to Kodiak Island, but Baranof wasn't there—he'd already reconquered Sitka. Before Rezanov went on to Sitka, he stored the materials for his university in a small, unused building at Kodiak."

"You never mentioned anything about a university."

"What do you mean I didn't?"

"You just didn't."

"The maps, the ship models, the scientific instruments, the books—I never mentioned all that?"

"I guess not."

Torsen looked doubtful. "More likely you weren't listening."

"It's not important."

"What do you mean it's not important? You think I'm crazy or something? You think I'm making this all up?"

His face was turning red. "Hold on, Tor. I didn't mean anything by it."

"By what?"

"I dunno," I said. "By whatever I said."

Torsen threw down his fork. "You're trying my patience, you know that?"

He was staring at me like he was thinking about retrieving that fork and sticking me with it.

"Really, Tor, I'm interested. I'm way interested."

"You've got me off my game," he sputtered. "Where was I?"

"When Rezanov got to Kodiak Island, Baranof wasn't there. He'd already returned to Sitka and reconquered it."

"Alright then, maybe you were listening. Rezanov sailed on to Sitka—actually, it was called New Archangel back then. Rezanov's first glimpse of Sitka would have been of the knoll commanding the approaches to the harbor, the old village site. Now it was bristling with twenty cannons.

"Alaska being so wild, Rezanov was amazed with what Baranof had been able to accomplish with little help from home. Baranof got most of his supplies for the colony's far-flung settlements by trading with the American merchants sailing out of Massachusetts and the native king in Hawaii.

"The winter of Rezanov's visit, 1805–1806, the Tlingits were waging guerrilla war up and down the southeast coast. They succeeded in wiping out the nearest Russian settlement, at Yakutat. At Sitka, where Baranof was expecting an attack at any moment, it became impossible to continue hunting and fishing, and there were four hundred mouths to feed. People were dying of scurvy. A winter gale took one of the few company ships, with no survivors. Baranof dispatched a sloop to Hawaii for food relief, but there was no guarantee it would return.

"Rezanov decided to take action. He would journey south for food supplies, expanding Russian territory while he was at it. His plan was to trade for food with the Indians of the Columbia River, in the wilds of what we now call Washington and Oregon. While he was there he would scout for the site to build a Russian outpost. If he kept pushing down the coast, he could scout a second site where wheat could be grown, on the fringes of the Spanish possessions in California. Every Russian in Alaska had a craving for bread.

"He set sail in late February in the *Juno*, a well-armed schooner he'd bought from a Yankee skipper who'd traded in Sitka in the fall. Rezanov loaded it with all sorts of trade goods and many of the gifts originally intended for the mikado of Japan. By the time he reached the mouth of the Columbia River, eight of his sailors had died of scurvy. The rest of the crew was in pitiful condition. Rezanov had to abandon his plan of crossing the bar and sailing up the Columbia to trade with the Indians."

"What bar? What do you mean by 'crossing the bar'?"

"The sandbar. Before the jetties were built in the twentieth century, the river dropped stupendous amounts of sand as it met the ocean. The channel where you entered the river was narrow, and its position was always shifting from one season to the next. In years to come, it would become known as the Graveyard of the Pacific."

"If Rezanov had tried it and wrecked, you would have never ended up with his journal."

"You got that right. Picture his situation. He was in

desperate straits. The nearest civilization was the Spanish mission in San Francisco Bay. He knew full well that Spain had declared California off-limits to foreigners. What was he going to do? He had to find food for Sitka. He sailed all the way down the coast—"

"Burying plaques as he went?"

"That's for me to know," Torsen snapped. "Holding his breath, Rezanov sailed into San Francisco Bay. He anchored close to the presidio and said his prayers, hoping to avoid a repeat of what happened in Japan.

"Lucky for him, the commander of the presidio, Arguello, was away at Monterey, down the coast, and so was the Spanish governor, Arillaga. Arguello's young son was in charge. The son allowed Rezanov to come ashore, and told him he could talk to his father and the governor when they got back from Monterey.

"The only man on Rezanov's ship who spoke Spanish was Rezanov himself. In the days before Arguello returned from Monterey, Rezanov spoke it often with the commander's beautiful fifteen-year-old daughter, Maria de la Concepcion Arguello, nick-named Concha."

"Aha, the plot thickens."

"Concha's father returned from Monterey to find that the foreigners had been made welcome. What's worse, his daughter had fallen deeply in love with Rezanov. Concha told her father that this was the man she would marry.

84

"Her father was plenty angry, but once he cooled down, he decided his daughter had chosen well. As for Rezanov, no question this was political as well as personal. He was picturing an alliance between Russia and Spain. The marriage would enable him to negotiate with Spain for the Pacific Northwest clear down to its northern outposts, two missions north of San Francisco."

"Would Spain have agreed to that?"

"Rezanov thought so; my hunch is, he was right. Spain was in a weakened position at the time. It knew it had more of the world than it could hang on to. The English and the Americans could be kept at bay if Spain and Russia worked together.

"There were complications. Rezanov and Concha weren't the same religion. With her father's approval, they were betrothed anyway, pending a dispensation from the pope and the approval of the king of Spain. Now that the Russian was virtually a relative, Arguello got Arillaga to agree to trade with Rezanov. The *Juno*'s trade cargo was off-loaded and replaced with wheat and beans and so on.

"The cloth-of-gold intended for the mikado of Japan went to Concha. Rezanov was able to return to Sitka in June with his precious cargo. He left for home as soon as he could, on fire to get back to St. Petersburg and the czar with all his news and his plans involving the Spanish. He lacked the ship, crew, and provisions that would have made it possible to sail home around

Asia and Africa, so he sailed to Siberia. He lost time outfitting a ship to make a raid that would punish Japan, then set out for St. Petersburg on horseback. It was a journey of thousands of miles with winter staring him in the face.

"Rezanov came down with pneumonia along the way. He holed up for five months and got started again in March of 1807. Weak and still sick, he fell from his horse and died from a head injury nearly four years after his journey began."

"What a story! What happened to Concha?"

"Legend has it she waited forty years for him, but the truth is, she found out about his death within six. She never married. In a trunk that Rezanov had left behind—a sea chest with the imperial double-headed eagle on the clasp—Concha put away the wedding dress she had made from the cloth-of-gold. She became a nun, and lived out her long life in a convent."

"What about the journal? Did she know about the journal hidden in the trunk?"

"Yes, she even wrote in it. She discovered the false bottom and the journal many years later, after California had passed from Spanish to Mexican to American hands. After the gold rush in 1849."

"Why did Rezanov leave the journal behind, if it had the locations of the plaques?"

"My guess is, he thought it would be useful when he returned to California. Who knows, he might have meant to take it out of the trunk before he left for Alaska, and forgot. At any rate, it's unlikely that his journal would have been the only record of the locations. Baranof would have had a record, at least of the ones planted between the Aleutians and Sitka in the late 1700s. Who knows, a record of the plaque locations might have been in Sitka when the Americans raised the Stars and Stripes in 1867. Some lout of an American lieutenant, who couldn't read the language, might have thought it was worthless Russian trash, and destroyed it."

"So, if Rezanov had lived, the history of the Northwest would have turned out all different."

"Russian America would have become something grand, I have no doubt of that. Rezanov would have seen the possibilities far beyond the trade in sea otter pelts. Alaska wouldn't have been sold off to the Americans, you can bank on it. Now, if you'll excuse me, it's past my bedtime."

A couple minutes later, the man was snoring.

11

T HE *STORM PETREL* WAS ON autopilot and we were
plowing north at six knots in heavy seas. "Is that
metallic taste in your mouth getting stronger?" I
asked at breakfast.

Tor looked at me like he had no idea what I was
talking about.

"Plaque Number 11?" I reminded him.

No response. After all of his storytelling the night
before, the well had apparently run dry. He was
making me feel like he regretted telling me about the
possession plaques, the trunk, the journal, all of it. It
was like he was a logger and I was a tree he was thinking about cutting down.

I didn't know what his problem was, I only wished

he didn't have one. Trying to cheer him up, I took a different tack: "How do you wake up exactly at four every morning without an alarm clock?"

"Just do."

"Are we dropping the gear today?"

"Likely not."

"No time to fish? How far are we headed?"

Torsen glared at me to remind me that I was on a need-to-know basis. "Cape Cross," he finally grunted.

I didn't dare ask if we were going there for the fishing or for treasure hunting. Tor was reaching for his Tylenol.

By midmorning Chichagof Island was in sight, off to our right. It's one of the biggest in Southeast, and on its windward side it has a convoluted shoreline, along with lots of timbered islands and rocky islets offshore. As we crawled the length of Chichagof, I turned to paging through Tor's books and studying the maps. In nine days we had come almost the entire length of Alaska's panhandle.

By evening we reached Yakobi Island, the farthest north and west of the eleven hundred islands in the Alexander Archipelago. A third of the way up its length, twenty miles or so, we anchored in a bay underneath Cape Cross. We would fish the cape the next day. It was another spot where Tor had knocked the kings dead in years past—ten thousand pounds once, from that one drag.

Along with seven other trollers, we fished it hard, fifteen hours, on July 10. The weather was foul. We caught only four kings and seven cohos. Since we'd sold on the fourth of July, we had caught a grand total of twenty-four kings and sixteen cohos. My share of the proceeds wasn't even worth calculating. Double earnings if we found a plaque wasn't all that exciting, either, two times zero being zero.

And so far we weren't even looking for a plaque, despite all Tor's talk.

Maybe he was just a con artist stringing me along with promises of a big paycheck. But why? And there was something about the way he was looking at me. I could feel him staring.

Maybe he thought I didn't believe his story. Or just the opposite: that I knew too much about his plans. Did he think I might tell someone? I hadn't had a chance to tell anyone, even if I'd wanted to.

Then it hit me hard. It didn't matter what I knew— if I never had a chance to tell anyone else.

I was scaring myself. It was the end of our tenth day out, but it seemed like I'd been away a whole lot longer. Time and space and reality were bent on this boat. Was I losing the ability to distinguish between what was real and what I was imagining? I had no idea what to make of Tor Torsen.

I would have been glad if the radio had announced the closing of king season, no matter that I'd go home barely better than broke. I was tired to the bone and homesick for Port Protection.

The morning of July 11, the other trollers took off

for the Fairweather Grounds to the north. There was talk on the squawk box about the fishing picking up there. I guessed we would follow suit, but I was mistaken. Instead of going out on the bow and pulling anchor, Tor went down in the engine room and brought up three items: a pick, a shovel, and a metal detector.

"You ready to dig?" he asked.

"Just tell me where," I said awkwardly.

"You're slow on the draw this morning."

"I'll have another cup of coffee. Where do we dig?"

"Out on the tip of the cape, but how close to the cape we can land, that's going to be the problem. So far I haven't seen a spot along the shore that will work."

We ate breakfast, and then the captain motored deeper into the bay. It was a raw, rainy, windy day, and the surf had teeth even on the somewhat protected underbelly of the cape. At last, four or five miles in, we came to a bit of a cove. "There." I pointed.

Tor shook his head. "It's got a little beach now, but at high tide, it'll be all rocks and driftpiles. Nowhere decent above the high tide line to leave the skiff."

"Down in the fo'c'sle, next to the survival suits, you've got an old rope net," I said.

"What about it?"

I explained what I had in mind, and Tor went for it. While he dropped anchor, I climbed up to the top of the wheelhouse where his little plastic landing skiff was rigged alongside the canister that stored the self-inflating life raft required by the Coast Guard. The skiff was so light, it was easy to lower it over the side. It had a pair of oars.

I placed the pick, shovel, and net inside, along with a coil of rope, my daypack, and an orange buoy that Tor used for one of his boat fenders. The daypack had enough snacks to get us through the day. For drinking water, there would be a creek every time we turned around.

"I'm going below," Tor announced. "You want one of those survival suits, just in case?"

"Maybe so, or else I'll never warm up after I swim."

Tor returned with the survival suit and a high-powered rifle, which gave me the jitters. He filled his shirt pockets from a box of shells.

"There's brownies up here," he explained with a slow grin as I began to put on the survival suit. Just like a dog, he had a way of smelling fear. "Brown bears, huge coastal grizzlies. Not your Prince of Wales black bears."

Torsen rowed us to shore. I was entertaining the fantasy of grabbing his rifle and tossing it into deep water. I made the landing off the bow, then collected four rocks the size of watermelons.

There was no cover on the small gravel beach. Tor huddled in the rain cradling his rifle and looking miserable. I draped my rain gear over my clothes, rubber boots, and daypack, and shoved off with the skiff.

Twenty yards offshore, I jury-rigged an anchor for the skiff with the net and the rocks. I attached the rope, lowered the anchor into twenty feet of water, then tied to the buoy. I swam back to shore and was happy for the survival suit. Only my hands and feet were freezing.

After ten days, my brain was so used to the around-the-clock rocking of the boat, now it was the land that was moving. Fast as I could in the rain, falling down twice, I got out of the survival suit and pulled on my socks and boots, jacket, raingear, and sou'wester hat in a rolling frenzy that had Torsen chuckling for the first time in days. "Let's get off the beach," he barked. "There's a solid wall of devil's club in our way. You first. You're the Alaskan."

12

THE BEACH GRAVEL WAS strewn with bull kelp, beached jellyfish, and broken shells of crabs and razor clams. The strip between the high tide line and the jumble of driftwood logs left by monster storms was littered with the usual pieces of Styrofoam. My eye went to a half-buried salmon flasher and a headless Barbie. Without even thinking about it—beachcombing was a lifetime habit—I kept scanning for man-made objects as I crawled over the logs to look for a way into the trees. You never knew what you might find.

A small bit of rounded green glass caught my eye. It was showing above the coarse gravel between two giant logs. I'd forgotten all about what my sister had told me at the last—to keep my eye out for a glass ball for her, and that's what this was. I fell to my knees and started digging with my hands. "What's going on?" Torsen yelled from the beach. I had dropped from sight, and he sounded suspicious.

"Nothing," I yelled back. "I found something." I kept digging like a bear starving for clams. Japanese fishermen used to use these virtually unbreakable glass balls as floats on their fishing nets. Every two or three years my family would come across one the size of a grapefruit. I'd seen one the size of a volleyball once, but today I couldn't believe my luck. The one I was holding in my hands was bigger than a basketball. This was the beachcombing trophy of a lifetime.

I heard Tor clambering over the logs, and now he stood high above me with his rifle. I held up the big green float; it didn't make him smile. "For my sister," I said, as his eyes appraised my prize.

"I'll consider it," he said. "I thought you were working for me. You have no idea how much I could get for that ball."

"I don't even want to know."

"Cutting you in for your fifteen percent, that would be fair enough, don't you think?"

"I don't care how much you could sell it for," I said stubbornly. "It's mine, for my sister, Maddie. Finders keepers—like your plaques, Tor."

He laughed. The way he laughed, the way he was holding the rifle, and the way he had me so far below him, between the gigantic logs: it flashed through my mind that this exact spot could be my grave.

"Leave it be for now," Torsen ordered. The rain, gusting off the cove, was dripping through his tree-moss beard. "We're burning daylight. I thought you had a job to do."

For now I just wanted off, off of Torsen's boat and out of his life. I wanted my old life back.

As I walked the high side of the drift logs looking for a way through the devil's club, I told myself that my sister would have the glass float in the end.

There's no part of devil's club that doesn't hurt. Six, eight, ten feet high, their stalks bristle with thorns. Even their foot-wide leaves are armored with stickers. I began to see a way through the jungle if I angled this way, then that.

I was less than halfway through when something in the trees behind the devil's club started huffing and snorting. I could hear it but I couldn't see it. I froze. It was getting closer. "Hey, bear," I said.

The noise stopped. Everything except for my heart went dead still.

"Hey, bear. Hey, bear." I was ready to bolt.

After a minute without hearing a thing, I thought I heard it moving away. After a couple of minutes without a sound I took a few cautious steps forward. The animal started snorting again, then gave a sharp woof.

That's it, I thought. I'd had enough. I turned and worked my way back to the beach, but a little too fast.

No wonder the side of my hand stung; it looked like a pincushion.

"What took you so long?" Tor growled as I began pulling stickers with my teeth.

"Didn't you hear anything?"

"Not a thing."

"Someone doesn't want us on this island. One of those brownies, I guess."

"Did you find a way through?"

"I think so."

"I'll lead, with the rifle."

"What do you say we try again tomorrow?"

"Go through all of this again? Are you nuts?"

"I just don't think we should shoot a bear if it isn't necessary."

"What are you, a tree hugger? Bear hugger? Go back and grab the pick and shovel, the metal detector, and the survival suit. Once we get through the devil's club, we'll hang the suit in a branch to mark our way back to this cove."

We never saw my bear. When we didn't even see tracks in the delicate, spongy moss on the far side of the devil's club, Tor looked at me like I was a five-year-old who'd hollered wolf. I shrugged. I didn't know what to think. I was remembering a native legend about forest creatures that are half animal, half human. When people drown and their bodies are never found, that's what happens to them. Get a grip, Robbie, I told myself.

Tor hung the bright orange survival suit in a tree. "Let's march," he said.

I stayed close behind the man with the gun. It was slow going, especially for me, carrying all the tools. We threaded our way among fifteen-foot root discs of blown-down Sitka spruce. Atop the lengths of the fallen giants, a new generation of trees was growing from the decay. How in the world was Torsen even going to put the metal detector to work? Two hundred years had gone by, enough time for a two-hundred-foot tree to grow right on top of the plaque. Or for one of these colossal trees to fall across the spot where Number 11 was buried.

From the branches above, the ravens were talking to us, or about us, with their gurgling and popping sounds. Midafternoon, we finally left the big trees behind and picked our way through a half mile of stunted spruce, hemlock, and yellow cedar that were windblown and leaning away from the ocean.

Finally we broke out into the open. We were standing high on Cape Cross, and could see up and down the coast. In both directions, the surf was battering the rocky shore. Here and there, jets of white shot up like geysers, and the spindrift rolled up the slopes to join the cloud vapor hanging in the trees. It was another scene my mother would have loved to paint.

Torsen switched on his metal detector and started walking slowly down the spine of the cape. He kept the machine close to the ground and swept its head slowly back and forth.

"I get it," I said. "The Russians planted the plaques out in front of where the trees grow, so it would be possible to find them."

"On the capes," Torsen said. "Number 12, at St. Michael's Redoubt, was an exception."

Torsen kept working his way down. Mostly it was smooth-scoured stone, with stunted knee-high trees growing in the crevices where pockets of soil had washed down from the forest above. Five, six times he had me dig where his metal detector did a little clicking. I produced nothing but holes.

Just before the cape's final drop into the sea, over a pocket of dirt covered only by moss, his metal detector went off like a rattlesnake.

I started to dig. Torsen grabbed the shovel away from me. "I don't want it damaged," he growled.

Six inches down, his shovel struck something solid. Torsen motioned for me to back off. He sat by the hole and dug with his fingers until he exposed the tops of what looked like bricks planted upright, two rows of three bricks with something sandwiched between. Something metal, also placed upright.

Torsen pulled the bricks out and then removed a plaque. He swept its surface with his fingers. Big as life, there was the double-headed eagle, and there was the number he was expecting, Number 11.

"Unreal," I said. "I can't believe what I've just seen with my own eyes."

"Believe it," Tor said. With the sleeve of his raincoat, he wiped the sandy mud off the plaque, then put the plaque to his lips and kissed it. "History," he cried out. "This is history you're looking at here, living history. You doubted me, boy, didn't you?"

"Did I say I did?"

"You didn't need to. Now, let's get out of here before dark catches us under the trees. You go in front."

"Why's that? You're the one with the gun."

"Exactly," he said with a laugh. "I'll cover you. You'll scare 'em off clinking and clanking with the tools."

None of this made any sense. Tor was giddy in a scary sort of way. All the way back, he raved about his good luck, how he had it coming after busting his hump his whole life.

He was so loud, I didn't have to worry about surprising a bear. It was Torsen I was worried about, his gun at my back. I should have recognized the signs back in Craig. The guy was mental.

Nobody would hear the gunshot. He'd bury me right where I'd found the glass float, just scoop out a shallow grave, throw me in and shovel the sand over me, then heave a log on top.

No, the bears had too keen a sense of smell, and they were carrion eaters. Torsen would know that. He would wrap my body in that fishing net along with those anchor rocks I had collected. Offshore, over deep water, he would drop me to the bottom of the ocean where the crabs would pick my bones clean.

A bullet could be traced to a firearm, I thought.

There was a much easier way. Offshore, when no boats were in sight, he could give me a shove into the Pacific anytime he wanted. In these waters, getting away with murder would be the easiest thing in the world. "The kid fell off while I was in the wheelhouse," Torsen would say. "I have no idea exactly when it happened. When I realized he wasn't on the boat, I turned back and searched, but—"

Maybe the plaques *weren't* finders keepers, like he claimed. Maybe he'd only hired me because I'd accidentally seen his illegal treasure. Because I might talk. I remembered how, after throwing me off his boat, he'd shown up at the pay phone just as I was about to make a call. He was all agitated about me making that call.

I had myself scared witless by the time we returned to what should have been the area where we'd first entered the forest. Once we got there, something was weird. The survival suit wasn't on the branch where Tor had left it, or anywhere nearby.

"What's the deal?" Tor said. "Did you put it somewhere when I wasn't looking?"

"I was with you the whole time. What are you talking about?"

"I don't remember," he claimed. "Maybe that's so, and maybe it's not so."

"Calm down," I said.

"Don't be telling me what to do."

"Let's look around. It must be close by." I had a plan, if only I could get a little distance on him. It was dusk. I could hide in the rain forest, hide so well he'd have no chance of finding me by dark. When he gave up and left with the *Petrel*, I'd flag another fishing boat.

"It's getting late, hard to see," I said. "Let's split up, we'll find it faster."

Torsen's eyes narrowed. He looked me up and down. "We'll stick together," he said, gesturing with the barrel of his gun. "I don't want you getting lost in the woods." He laughed.

After tromping all around, we finally found the survival suit, well back in the trees. It had been torn to shreds. This time the bear tracks were unmistakable.

I had to swim out to the skiff without a survival suit. It took only a couple minutes, but I was shivering cold as I hauled myself aboard. "Just untie from the buoy if the anchor is too heavy," Tor called.

"I think I can pull it up," I said, stalling for time. I was thinking about trying to ditch him. Just leave him on the island.

Maybe not, I decided as I heaved up the anchor. He had the rifle. He'd have me dead to rights.

"What's the matter with you?" Tor said when I bumped the shore, and he stepped into the skiff with the rifle and the glass float. "Seen a sea monster? You don't look so good."

"I'm cold," I said, which was partly true.

13

THE WIND QUIT THAT NIGHT. I was so used to the rocking of the boat, the stillness startled me awake. At first I had no idea where I was, and then I remembered. I was aboard the *Storm Petrel*, and I wanted off.

It was twenty after three by my watch. I had too much to worry about, and couldn't get back to sleep. Forty-five minutes later, the captain's mental alarm clock woke him up. As he was pulling anchor, I was already making the coffee. Tor had turned the VHF up loud, and it was blaring the weather forecasts from Yakutat clear down to Dixon Entrance.

"Let's pull the stabilizers," Torsen called from the wheelhouse door. "We'll go faster with them out of the water."

I thought I knew what this meant: in a few minutes I'd be homeward bound. "Heading south?"

"Not on your life. Look, it's flat as a griddle out there. Winds light to variable on the Fairweather Grounds for the foreseeable future, that's what they're saying. I thought you wanted to catch fish until your arms fall off."

"Won't it take a long time to get there?"

"It's another day north."

"What if Fisheries closes the season right after we get to the Fairweather Grounds?"

"What if they don't? This is a fishing boat, or haven't you noticed? It's always a gamble. Last year, king season stayed open sixteen, seventeen days. My guess is, we get in at least three days fishing up there. Three days is a lifetime if they're biting."

"Do we have enough gas?"

He looked at me as if to ask what business that was of mine, then said, "We'll take a different route back. We can gas and sell at Pelican."

Tor bent to pull the starboard stabilizer. I did the same on my side. As it cleared the water, I cranked hard on the rope to bring it above the bulwark. The stabilizer is a sort of flying wedge suspended by a rope from the middle of the trolling pole, one on each side of the boat. They ride two fathoms under the surface and reduce the side-to-side rocking of the boat. They also steady the action of the lures trailing behind. You don't want to drop one on your foot; there's a sawed-off cannonball welded to the underside.

As I grappled with mine and lowered it to the deck, I heard Tor cry out. His stabilizer hit the deck with a thud and his hand went to his lower back. His face was contorted with pain. "Now I've done it," he roared. "Now I've done it."

"I should have gotten both of them," I said lamely.

"Too late now," he said through clenched teeth as he staggered into the wheelhouse.

I followed, hoping this meant we couldn't go farther north after all.

Tor sat on the edge of his bunk, grimacing when he wasn't cursing under his breath. He had me get some pills from his things, a bottle of prescription painkillers that his daughter, Grace, had sent with him just in case. He took two.

The engine was running; we were adrift. "What now?" I ventured.

"Grab your coffee and slide in behind the wheel. Put it in gear and throttle up. Let's get out of here."

"Head south?"

"North! We already settled that. You signed up for king season, not a part of it. I thought you wanted to make some money!"

"I did, but your back—"

"There's no buts when you've got a weather forecast like this. My whole life, I never lost a day's fishing to aches and pains. Listen carefully: I want you to steer dead center out of this bay before heading north. Watch the Fathometer close, and use the GPS to follow the fifty-fathom contour around Cape

Cross. Tell me when we're in the clear."

I did what I was told.

"Okay," I said fifteen minutes later. "The cape is due starboard."

"The next GPS cassette is in the drawer. It's got the Fairweather Grounds on it."

"Okay, got it. There, it's on the screen. No more islands north of us, just the mainland coast."

"That's right, the St. Elias Mountains."

"I can see 'em out the window, in the distance."

"A white wall, right?"

"I've never seen anything like it in my life."

"Three miles high and practically straight up. Keep scanning north on the GPS until you get to Cape Spencer and Lituya Bay."

"Got those."

"Look forty miles offshore. You'll find the Fairweather Grounds."

"Forty miles offshore? I thought the Fairweather Grounds must be off of Cape Fairweather."

"You thought wrong. They're called the Fairweather Grounds because on a clear day like today, you can see Mount Fairweather from there. Just like Captain Cook did when he named the sucker. Foulweather would have been more accurate. I've seen the peak only three, maybe four times."

"Okay, I've located the Fairweather Grounds. From the contours, it looks like an underwater mountain range."

"That's exactly what it is. There's the west bank

and the east bank, with a wide gully in between. At one point you're only seventy-eight fathoms above a peak. Swarms of salmon feed—herring and needle-fish—hang out in the nooks and crannies. No end of kings there if you hit it just right, like we aim to. Punch in the coordinates for the southern end of the grounds. Then punch us a course from here to there, direct. No need to hug the coast on a day like this."

"Did it," I reported a couple minutes later. "We're on autopilot, navigating by satellite."

It gave me a queasy feeling to be putting the land at my back. If I had reason to be afraid of Torsen, I was doing exactly the wrong thing. Too late now. "I'll make some breakfast," I announced.

"Watch out some freighter doesn't run us down."

"Are you feeling better?"

"I'll get up for breakfast."

"Coffee, now?"

"What, drink it on my back? How fast you got us going?"

"Nine knots."

"Leave it at that."

I fried some bacon and made French toast with the last of our bread. Tor sat at the edge of his bunk as I set out the food, along with orange juice and coffee. He got up very carefully, but even so he was staggered by another bolt to his lower back. After steadying himself, he gritted his teeth, cursed, and settled into the aft side of the table where he could look over the bow.

Tor kept looking past me as he nibbled at a piece of

bacon. His eyes were on the horizon though there was nothing to be seen. His face was unreadable as ever, like time-weathered stone.

The minutes went by like slowly dripping water. I couldn't take the silence. "So where do you run to for the night," I asked, "when you're fishing the Fairweather Grounds?"

"You don't," he said impatiently. "You drift."

"Just drift?"

"Just drift. Sometimes you end up miles from where you started."

"What if some big ship comes through when you're sleeping?"

"You hope they see your light."

"Sounds a little sketchy."

"It is, but it's worth it. It's big-time fishing."

"What happens if the weather turns on you? Where's your protection?"

"If the weather's not too rough, you can ride it out on the lee side of Cape Fairweather. If it's bad, you head into Lituya Bay."

"I think I've heard of Lituya Bay."

He looked like he was going to say something. "You may have," was all he said. He got up, stiff as a robot. Having left most of what was on his plate, in seconds he was flat on his back again.

Midmorning, and there still wasn't a cloud in the sky—freakish weather for Southeast. The flatness of the sea amplified the vastness. Unlike the sea bird it was named after, the *Storm Petrel* couldn't take to the air if things turned ugly. It was going to be exciting to fish the open ocean, like a big-time Alaska commercial fisherman. Maybe too exciting. I'd heard plenty of stories, and I'd seen videos of storms in the Gulf of Alaska. At forty-five feet, the *Storm Petrel* was a big boat compared to my family's *Chimes of Freedom*, but it was still classified as a small craft when it came to weather advisories.

Well, here I was, way, way outside and more scared than I'd expected to be. My biggest consolation, ironically, was my skipper. Tor had lived to be a graybeard, which meant my chances of getting home in one piece were good to excellent.

Unless he didn't want me to.

Tor got up for lunch, and this time he stayed up. He suddenly remembered to double-check the course I had charted. I was relieved to find we were on target for the Fairweather Grounds, and not China.

Torsen read a gloomy article about the future of wild salmon in his Alaska fishing journal, the *Pilothouse Guide*. I looked through his bookshelf for something on Lituya Bay, with a strong suspicion that it was known for something. I couldn't seem to remember.

At last I found some photographs of the bay along with a note about what it was famous for: an earthquake late in the evening of July 9, 1958. The quake's epicenter was in the mountains at the head of the narrow bay.

I could barely believe what I was reading. The

mountain to the edge of the glacier at the head of the bay sloughed so much rock, so fast, that the splash reached 1,720 feet up the opposite ridge across the narrow arm of the back bay. In one fell swoop, the wave scoured every tree and every bit of soil off that slope, from sea level to seventeen hundred feet up. The photographs proved the unimaginable. Before, all trees. After, nothing but bedrock.

"Look at this," I said.

"Yeah," Tor replied. "Lituya Bay. Did you read about the trollers?"

"There's nothing here about trollers. Were there some in the bay when it happened?"

"Three trollers had anchored for the night, two just inside the spit at the entrance of the bay and one a mile or so inside, on the south side. A giant swell from the big splash raced down the bay at a hundred miles an hour, something like that. The people in the boats, they'd heard the big landslide and could see the swell coming. The boat farthest inside the bay rode way up on it and washed back safely. The other two, at full throttle, tried to ride the wave out of the bay."

"You're kidding."

"You look a little green around the gills. You should. Be scared, kid: you have no idea what the ocean can do. When the swell hit the spit of land that pinches the mouth of Lituya down to a small opening onto the Pacific, that's where it rose the highest, and that's where it crested and broke. Both of the trollers that took the ride were destroyed."

"Any survivors?"

"One crew was lost, one survived—a married couple. They told of looking down from the crest of the wave onto the tops of trees eighty feet below. When their troller was swamped outside the spit, they managed to climb into their skiff."

"Unbelievable."

"Believe it."

"Wait a minute, Tor. It says here that on average, an earthquake wave in Lituya Bay occurs every twenty-two years. It says a wave drowned a party of Tlingits once, in their war canoes. Didn't you say that Lituya Bay was our safe harbor? With a wave more than twenty years overdue?"

The old pirate grinned through his pain. "Feeling lucky?"

14

SALMON TROLLERS DOTTED the northern horizon. We had reached the west bank of the Fairweather Grounds. To the east, one mountain peak stood higher than all the rest along the great white wall. "When you can see Mount Fairweather," Tor said, "you've got a couple days of fair weather fishing ahead of you."

"If we can't see it, we don't stay here?"

"I didn't say that. You fish it anyway, you just don't sleep as easy. You listen to the forecasts, and you watch the birds, the clouds, and your barometer, in case you have to make a run for it."

At last we closed with the boats ahead. Tor throttled down and we dropped in behind a troller heading north. Two men were leaning over the stern, gaffing salmon. I said, "You see what I see?"

"Drop the gear," Torsen answered. "We got three hours of daylight. Make it count."

I swung into the cockpit and let the gear down, port side first. Torsen stood above, hanging on to the hayrack and watching my every move.

Let him watch. The bite was on, and I was ready to do some serious fishing. I had worse things to fear from him than making a mistake running his gear.

I didn't have to wait long. The tip line was jerking before I even put the heavy down.

"Never had trouble with sea lions out here," Tor said. "Run all four lines down before you start to pull any back up. I'll steer from up front. You're going to have to do all the fishing."

"I can handle it," I said as I began to bring the first line up. There was a king on the second leader, and underneath it, another on the third.

Until it was getting too dark to see, nearly four hours later, I ran the gurdies, clubbed and gaffed and landed and cleaned salmon. It was unbelievable, and they never quit coming. Afterward, by the electric lights in the fish hold, I iced them until there wasn't another left to be taken care of. At last I climbed out of the hold, shucked my gory bibs and boots, and staggered into the wheelhouse.

Torsen was snoring. My watch said ten minutes after eleven. I flicked the switch above the galley sink and looked at myself in the mirror. My face was speckled with dried fish blood. There were fish scales on the tip of my nose; a piece of gut was stuck to the side of my chin. I was sunburned and my hair was matted with slime.

Torsen's dirty dishes were in the sink. The man hadn't forgotten whose job that was, I thought bitterly. He could have left me something to eat.

I stared dully at my forearms. Washing the dishes would rid me of the scales glued to my skin. They were thick as sea lice around the vent of a salmon.

I needed to refuel my body first, then do the dishes, but was about to give up on all of it. Then I spotted a pan covered with aluminum foil at the side of the stove—baked salmon and a baked potato. I wolfed it down, desperate to get some sleep. On my way below, I hit the switch to turn off the wheelhouse lights. At the last second I remembered the fish-hold lights. Tor would definitely kill me, I thought with a grim laugh, if he woke to a dead battery.

In less than an hour it would be day thirteen. My parents and my sister would have gone out on two or three short trips during this time. Back home we never fished more than three days in a row. I could picture my family clean and showered and sleeping at home.

I went down the ladder and collapsed in my bunk.

Man, I needed a hot shower. My clothes stank, I stank, the boat stank. Drifting in the dark forty-eight miles from shore, it was insane. But working four lines the way I had done, doing all that work all by myself, what a rush that had been. Day thirteen, bring it on. I'll do the same, slaughter them from dawn to dark. I was making money now, real money.

It was the sound of the squawk box, turned all the way up, that woke me. Why not the anchor chain, I wondered for a second, then remembered we weren't anchored. It was 4:00 A.M.

I pulled on my clothes and staggered up the ladder, afraid that the weather was changing. "What's the barometer doing?" I asked first thing.

"Check for yourself."

I did. "It's staying up. More good weather, like you said. Can you see Fairweather?"

"Don't know yet."

"Not enough daylight, eh?" My laugh sounded forced, because it was.

"Make yourself a cup of coffee to take back to the cockpit with you. Grab a box of cookies."

"You're kidding. It's too dark to fish."

"Do the dishes first, then. I never kid about fishing."

"I forgot all about the dishes. It was late."

"Hurry up. In a few minutes, it'll be light enough to see the gear."

"How far did we drift? Aren't we off the grounds?"

"We drifted eight miles. We're over the western edge of the east bank."

I stumbled out onto the deck and relieved myself over the side. I could see mast lights from close to twenty trollers, but nobody was fishing yet.

Washing my hands and my face at the galley sink, I felt semihuman again. After nearly two weeks with little sleep, I was punch-drunk, like a brain-injured boxer. I did the dishes, then made myself a mug of coffee, double strong.

Torsen seemed to be sizing me up, like a trainer from the corner of the ring. He was wondering if I was going to make it through round thirteen.

"Lemme at 'em," I said. "How's your back?"

"Still locked up. Pills don't even touch it. Barely slept." Torsen hit the starter button and the *Storm Petrel*'s engine rumbled to life. As it warmed up, I went through my mug of coffee and five cookies, then fixed another mug.

"Ready when you are," Tor said.

I took my coffee and cookies with me, dropped into the cockpit, set the treats aside, and began to put the gear down. Before I got a chance to take another slug of coffee, the poles started rattling, and they never quit. Five hours later, I stumbled into the wheelhouse for breakfast.

"Now, that was some fishing," Torsen said over bacon and eggs and home fries.

"You're keeping the count, right?"

"Since we got here, it's a hundred and forty-three kings and seventy-seven cohos."

"Is the mountain out? I forgot to look."

"It's in the cirrus clouds."

"How's the barometer?"

116

"Showing high pressure. Steady at thirty and a half."

"How about the forecast?"

"Yakutat to Cape Spencer, winds white to terrible."

It took me a couple of seconds to be startled. "What did you say?"

"Easy, sailor. It's a joke, an old fisherman's joke. I'm surprised you don't know it. They're saying 'Winds light to variable.' The guy in the nice warm office can't always be believed, but that's what he's saying. We'll keep checking the other signs."

"Good. I'll fish, you steer and keep an eye on the weather."

Suddenly the tinkling of bells from the tattletales started up again. I grabbed my rubber gloves. "Starboard tip and port heavy," Torsen said.

It got crazy again. All day it rained salmon onto the bloody deck of the *Storm Petrel*. In my wildest dreams I had never imagined it could be like this. I didn't get to bed until midnight.

I'd have accomplished everything I'd set out to do, if only I made it off that boat and back to Port Protection.

15

WOKE TO THE POSSIBILITY that king season might be called to a close any time now. Torsen, before he fell asleep, had heard the rumors on the VHF. All the fishermen were talking about it.

"What about the weather forecast?" I asked.

"Winds light to variable, with patches of sunshine. The wind shouldn't blow more than ten or fifteen knots. There's a couple of low pressure centers spinning around in the gulf. For the time being, they aren't moving this way."

The morning bite was hot and heavy. Then, mercifully, it shut off. I got the opportunity to catch up with the cleaning and put another forty-two salmon on ice.

As I stumbled into the wheelhouse, Torsen glanced

in my direction. He had a big wad of steel wool in his right hand; he'd been rubbing something with it. The plaque we'd found, I realized as I came a little closer. Number 11. There were shiny places where he'd been polishing. Individual feathers were showing up in the eagle's wings, as well as some major features that had been unrecognizable before.

I didn't say anything. I went to the galley sink and got to work with the soap and water. I raked my fore-arms with my fingernails, stripping off scales. "I'll get up and make us some breakfast," I heard Tor say. "You take a breather."

"Good deal," I said. He must have been feeling better, though he didn't say so.

I sat where Tor had been sitting, with my back to the galley, so I could look over the bow and cross quickly to the wheel in case of a close encounter with one of the oncoming trollers. There were eight within sight.

Tor had left the plaque right there on the table. "You can see a lot more detail now," I remarked.

"Quite the craftsmanship."

"What kind of metal?"

"Bronze or brass, maybe? It's got copper in it, I'm sure of that."

As the bacon began to pop and sizzle behind me, I had the feeling that this was a good thing, him want-ing to talk. "What's with the double-headed eagle?" I asked. "You said the Tlingits got it from the Russians. Where did the Russians get it?"

"From the Romans, strangely enough. The legions

of the Roman Empire marched behind an eagle symbol on a staff. In the later centuries, there was one emperor in Rome and another in Byzantium. The double-headed eagle was the symbol of the eastern emperor."

"Each of these eagle heads has a crown on it."

"The head looking west, that's Rome; the one looking east, that's Byzantium. After Rome fell, there was only the eastern empire, only the one emperor. Byzantium, eventually renamed Constantinople, finally fell in the mid-fourteen-hundreds. A couple decades later, the ruler of Moscow, Ivan, married the niece of the last eastern emperor. Now, you tell me why he did that."

"Because she was a babe?"

I didn't look over my shoulder to see the scowl. Torsen just kept going: "It was so he could proclaim himself heir to the Byzantine throne. He took on all the trappings and symbols, including the double-headed eagle. Even named himself czar, which came from the word *Caesar*."

"What about the shield in the middle of the eagle's body? I can't quite make it out, but it looks kind of like St. George slaying the dragon."

"That's exactly what it is. St. George was the patron saint of Moscow and Russia in general. In the eagle's talons on one side, that sword represents royal power, and on the other here, the orb with the cross on top, that represents the divine right of kings."

"This Number 11, at Cape Cross, it must have been buried before Rezanov went to San Francisco."

"That's right. Back in 1787, the Russian governor in the Siberian far east ordered a pair of navigators to bury the first five. In 1790, Baranof was given some more to bury as he expanded the colony around the shores of Alaska. How many, we don't know exactly. On his first recon of Sitka Sound, in 1795, was probably when he buried the one found at St. Michael's Redoubt. The Russians kept burying plaques along the coast until 1811, as they explored south from Sitka."

"So, this Number 11 we're looking at was probably buried by Baranof in 1795, on the same expedition when he planted Number 12?"

"That's what Rezanov says in his journal, and I have no reason to doubt him."

"On that journey to San Francisco, did Rezanov bury any more?"

"Of course. He was an expansionist. He was just as eager to plant possession plaques as he was to scout sites for new Russian outposts and to bring food back to Sitka."

"And nobody in the world knows about Rezanov's journal but you?"

"My buyer, he knows I've got it. And you do, Robbie Daniels. *You do*," he repeated as he took the plaque from the table and placed it under the mattress, at the foot of his bunk, next to Number 13.

His emphasis on those last two words was followed by silence, except for the whine of the wind outside.

Torsen returned with a platterful of breakfast and

set it in the center of the table. "Orange juice?" he barked.

"Yes, please."

When he'd set out the plates, silverware, and juice, and replenished the coffee, he sat down across from me, stared at me, right in the eye, and said, "What am I going to do with you?"

"What do you mean?" I asked as innocently as I could.

"You should never have come aboard my boat without permission."

He was agitated again, just like at the first, at the dock in Craig. "I know," I said. "I thought I told you I was sorry about that."

"Sorry? This is my whole retirement we're talking about here, what I can make from these plaques. Fishing, I can't do that anymore."

"Because of your back?"

He waved his fork at me. "That's just part of it. My whole livelihood is being destroyed right before my eyes! As if all the logging and the dams weren't bad enough. This salmon farming, it's got us fishermen on the short road to oblivion."

"I know," I said. "My parents are really worried, too. Our cash economy comes from the salmon runs in the Sumner Strait, pinks and sockeyes and cohos. Those salmon farms in British Columbia and Washington State, some of 'em have half a million salmon in one row of pens."

"Right, and salmon farming is supposed to double

in the next five years. Think what that'll do to the price of our wild salmon. The ocean is being strip-mined of crabs and small fish to feed all these farmed Atlantic salmon, and the feed pellets are laced with antibiotics, hormones, and red dye. Raising salmon in confinement, like they were pigs or chickens, bioengineering them to grow faster than nature intended—it's an unnatural scheme driven by greed, and it disgusts me."

"Most people don't know what's going on, Tor. When people eat Atlantic salmon, they don't even know that it's farmed. My dad says they're eating a drug-addicted couch potato instead of a healthy marathon runner, only they don't realize it. There's even health warnings about how many you should eat—on account of the toxins, can you believe that? People don't have any idea that huge numbers of farmed fish escape—how much of a dent that puts in the wild salmon's feed and habitat. And then there's the problem with the salmon lice. They multiply like crazy in the sewage around the fish farms. Those lice are killing the wild salmon before they get any bigger than your little finger."

"Us and the wild salmon, we're both dying breeds, kid, and let me tell you something: people don't care. After a lifetime of putting food on people's tables, we fishermen will disappear without so much as a thank-you. How is a man supposed to make a living, ever have a chance to retire? 'Isn't that quaint,' that's all people will say. 'Another vanishing way of life.'"

"You sound so bitter, Tor."

"Well, I am bitter!" he stormed. "My whole life, I've risked myself in the most dangerous profession in the world. If I need a back operation, who's going to pay for that? With the prices being driven so low, I'm not even going to get the chance to keep fishing. Anytime now, my costs will be more than I can make, no matter how good a fisherman I am. Guys are already being forced out in droves."

"Maybe something can still be done."

"It's already too late! It's terminal! What chance would I have to maintain my independence if that trunk hadn't come along, the Russian trunk, and Rezanov's journal, and these plaques? None!"

Torsen's eyes were wild, and trained right on me. I couldn't tell which way to turn, only that I had to convince him I was his ally. "It's lucky for you about the treasure laws," I said.

"What?" Torsen snapped.

"I mean, like when treasure hunters find Spanish galleons that went down in the Caribbean, like you said a while back. They get to keep the gold."

"Is that what you think?"

"Well, sure," I said as convincingly as I could.

"But when you get back home, and start asking questions, you'll find it's not so simple."

"Really, Tor, I don't know anything about it."

Tor slammed his knife on the table. "They'll tell you the plaques don't belong to me. But I deserve a break in life. I didn't ruin the fishing. I didn't drive the prices down."

"Sure, Tor, I understand."

"Do you?" he spat. "I suppose your parents will, too." His stare was loaded with menace. I felt my temperature rising.

"I won't tell a soul about the plaques," I said. "Look, you don't have to worry about me."

"You never should have come aboard without permission," he said, shaking his head. He said it gravely, like a judge pronouncing sentence.

Outside, the wind had been picking up. The sea was a stampede of white horses. My emotions were running just as wild. Tor was threatening me, no doubt about it. He'd made up his mind.

I got up without saying a word. I didn't want to look at him, didn't want him to smell my fear.

"Where you going?" he growled.

"Fishing," I called over my shoulder.

"It's too windy."

I reached for my rubber gloves. "The gauge is reading twenty-five knots. You said twenty-five was fishable."

My heart was still thundering when I reached the open air. I took some deep breaths, feeling like I'd been stunned by a gaff club. I reeled across the rolling deck and dropped into the cockpit. Working, that was the only way I was going to be able to handle this.

16

N THE WIND, THE LEADERS were quick to fly off the
stern, where I arranged them as I took them off the
trolling wire. They'd get tangled and I would lose
time. Whenever I managed to get the gear down,
though, I pulled kings, lots and lots of kings.

The afternoon brought flurries of rain. Tor, standing at the wheel, had taken us off autopilot. Trolling
north, before the wind, it was impossible to steer a
straight drag. The *Storm Petrel* would crab one way,
then the other, going up and down with the seas like a
yo-yo. Tor had to attend to the throttle as much as the
wheel. If the lures and flashers aren't traveling the
right speed, you won't catch fish. At the stern, the following seas would roll up on me like they might break

over the rail and into the cockpit. They nearly did.

When Tor would swing around and tack against that southeasterly wind, he had an easier time of it keeping the speed constant. I landed twice as many fish.

In a mindless sort of mechanical frenzy, I brought in phenomenal numbers, a couple hundred kings. When I had to work on deck to remove the salmon from the rinse tub, drop them into the hold, and refill the tubs with rinse water, it was all I could do to keep from being swept into the ocean. My knees ached from all the bracing. Tor, at the wheel, wasn't looking out for me, not that anyone could, from inside. He would never know if I went overboard.

Let the sea take him, is that what he was thinking? "The kid worked hard, but he had no judgment," that's what he would say.

The rest of the day, we didn't exchange more than a couple syllables. I watched my back and kept working. If it came to grappling with him, if he tried to throw me over the side, I was going to be ready. It was still difficult for him to move. He wouldn't be able to muster near his usual leverage.

Sometimes the squalls came hard, and the rain found my skin. If it weren't for my thermal clothing and the heat that came from battling the salmon, I would have frozen. My fingers were painfully cold. Every so often, despite the excellent fishing, one of the other trollers would break ranks and run toward land. "We'll leave the grounds to you highliners," they seemed to be saying. "More power to you."

Tor heard the announcement when I was working late, in the hold. King season would close at midnight on July 16. Two more days, that's what was left of this marathon. Tor intended to fish it down to the wire, that much was obvious.

Our kings, on average, were a little heavier than the ones we sold to the *Angie*. Tor was making about fourteen dollars a fish.

And I was making two bucks and change. That was good money, astounding money for a kid from Protection, if I lived to collect it.

The morning of day fifteen found the wind blowing out of the southwest instead of the southeast, and not nearly as hard. The sky was streaked with high cirrus; the rain was gone. The only problem was, the barometer was falling. I pictured one of those storms out in the gulf spinning in our direction. "What do you think about the barometer?" I asked. "It's below thirty."

I heard the alarm in my voice, and so did Torsen. "Sure is," he said, staring at me like I was the unsolvable puzzle, when it was the other way around.

"Okay, I'm jumpy, I admit it. I've never been so far from land. What are the weather guys in the warm office saying?"

"Same old, same old, through tomorrow: 'Winds light to variable, Yakutat to Cape Spencer.'"

"If the barometer's falling, how could the forecast be the same for tomorrow?"

"Don't be such a nervous Nellie, kid. Grab your

coffee and some cookies. Let's get the gear down. You might break eight hundred today."

"Eight hundred what?" I asked dully.

"Kings, just since we got here. How is space holding out below?"

"Still got some, but we're filling up. You figure we'll fish all the way through to dark tomorrow night?"

"Why wouldn't we?" the highliner barked. "Aren't you making money? Isn't that what you wanted?"

"Sure," I said. "I guess that's what it's all about."

"You make money, I make money, we're both happy."

If only he believed it was that simple.

That fifteenth day, the salmon ran in rivers out of the sea and onto the decks of the *Storm Petrel*. I was in such a killing frenzy, I was able to conk, gaff, and land them virtually in one motion. With the winds light, Torsen had us on autopilot and didn't need to stay behind the wheel. Instead he hung on the hayrack above me, his face a tight mask of pain, and watched me fish.

When I had to climb out of the cockpit to work on deck, to grab salmon from the rinse tubs and drop them in the hold, coming close to him was unavoidable. At all times, I tried to stay just out of reach. I was wary as a deer dropped in a pen with a lion. If he rushed me, I planned to sidestep and sweep him into the ocean. If it was going to be me or him, I was going to make sure it was him.

I kept clubbing my way through the kings. I thought there wasn't a salmon in the Gulf of Alaska that could match my fury, but I was wrong. Midafternoon, I was bringing up one of the lines when a fish all out of proportion to the rest I had caught appeared from the dark green depths. "You see the second one down?" I hollered over my shoulder. Tor was still hanging on the hayrack.

"Sure do," Tor replied.

"Can that be a king?" I yelled as I brought in the one above, whacked it, gaffed it, and swung it into the cleaning bin.

"Sure is," Torsen said. "You're going to have a battle on your hands. We don't want to lose that puppy."

"I don't aim to."

"It might run eighty or ninety pounds. They don't hardly get any bigger."

I took a deep breath and reached for the gurdy lever. I brought the steel line up, unsnapped the nylon leader, then slammed it onto the catch in the gear tray as fast as I could. I looked up as the enormous king, a tyee in the true sense of the word, leaped clean out of the ocean.

Hand over hand, I tried to draw the prize in. The fish was so strong, it took line from me as it torpedoed back and forth across our wake. "Send it back down and tire it out?" I yelled over my shoulder.

"No, no, bring it in or you'll lose it! Do I have to do it myself?"

I gritted my teeth, braced, and pulled harder. "No chance!"

The battle was only getting started. Three times, I had the fish nearly close enough to club. Three times, I leaned over the stern with the gaff club poised, only to have the king, in a splashing frenzy, take line away from me. It seemed to have a lot more strength left than I did. It was all I could do not to let up for an instant. A moment's slack and the tyee would be gone.

The fourth time, eye to eye, I anticipated the explosion that would come as the fish saw me raise my club. I bent my left wrist so the king couldn't pull the line straight out of my palm, and I held tight. With the club in my right hand, I came down hard, striking the giant salmon square on the top of the head. From the vibration in my elbow, it felt like I'd connected with concrete.

Now came the supreme test. Was I strong enough to land the thing? Once I committed, I was going to have to give it my all, and then some.

The time is now, I decided grimly. I spun the gaff in my hand, slammed the gaff hook through the side of the salmon's shaking head, then braced and heaved the giant up and over the rail. Just enough of its body fell into the bin for the momentum to bring the rest with it. Not for a second did it just lie there. Immediately, the great fish was beating its tail, slamming the bin, writhing and flopping every which way, so violently it nearly flopped over the side of the boat.

Quick as I could, I jerked the hook loose, then clubbed the salmon two times and once more for good measure.

"Ninety-five pounds if it weighs an ounce," Tor said. I stood back panting, exhausted.

As if the school underneath us was scattered and demoralized by the loss of its chieftain, the bite paused, and for that I was grateful. Tor went back into the wheelhouse. No doubt his back was killing him.

The mammoth king lay still, gasping, its jaws working open and shut. I turned my face away from its fading glory, and went to the other side of the cockpit to clean fish. I needed to give the tyee ten minutes to fully die before I could safely deal with it. There still might be enough life or reflex left in that fish to break my arm or worse.

Everybody in Southeast knew the story of Joe Cash, the troller who landed a halibut over the side of his boat, a hundred-thirty pounder, only to slip on the slimy deck and bang his head on a winch. There the man was, all alone, lying unconscious in the bin with the dying halibut. The thrashing of the fish broke Joe's leg so bad, the bone ruptured an artery. When he came to, he had lost so much blood, he didn't quite make it to his radio before he died.

I sprayed my smaller kings clean, heaved them forward into the port rinse bin, then crossed to the starboard side to work on the chieftain. It was so heavy, it was all I could do to pick it up and center it in the cleaning cradle, which it dwarfed.

I severed the gill connections, ripped the gills out, and tossed them over the side. Out spilled the salmon's still-beating heart and a handful of needlefish from the cut throat. I held the king's heart in my palm and felt a huge sadness wash over me.

If you do it with reverence, I reminded myself, there's no reason to be sad. That's what my parents had taught me.

With a flick of my wrist, I tossed the heart to the sea. A gull caught it before it hit the water.

Sometimes the needlefish were still alive, still bright-eyed and wriggling. I would flick them into the ocean, hoping they would live. These were dead.

As I slid the tip of the long, sharp cleaning knife into the vent of the enormous king salmon, it jerked, from reflex. It always bothered me that there's no way to know at what point the fish is truly dead and incapable of feeling pain.

I opened the cavity, ripped out the gut package and tossed it over the side to the screaming gulls. A few landed on it at once.

I sliced the blood canal along the length of the backbone, flipped the knife around, and stripped the congealing blood with the spoon on the other end. I reached for the deck hose and rinsed the inside of the fish with salt water.

Tor was above me again, leaning on the hayrack, looking down. Fishing had been his life. He must be feeling reverence, same as me, for this magnificent creature. I wished he felt the same reverence for his

Russian plaques, and Rezanov's journal. If he did, he'd never take them for himself, or sell them on the black market. He'd share them with the world instead.

The fishing picked up again, and I landed fish like there was no tomorrow. We had over fifteen thousand pounds of king salmon in the hold, not to mention the silvers. The trollers kept thinning out as the barometer continued to fall. By early evening there were only three boats in sight. With a couple of hours of daylight left, Torsen told me to pull the gear.

"Can we reach land?" I asked. "In case the weather comes up overnight?"

"And have to run back out to the grounds for the last day?" he answered with a scowl. "I'm talking about moving over to the east bank, that's all. Lituya Bay will be in better reach if we need to run there. Don't be in such a hurry to tuck tail. Don't you want to see what the outside water can do when it's riled up?"

"Not really," I said. "I wouldn't think you would, either."

"I've seen it all, kid, I've already seen it all."

I had hundreds of fish to deal with before I could sleep. It was dark by the time I got to the dishes. Tor was snoring. My sights were set on home; that was all I really cared about. My body felt like raw meat pounded with a hammer. My mind was rum-dumb from exhaustion.

Every night on the *Storm Petrel*, what sleep I got came to a screeching halt after a handful of hours, either with the anchor chain or the blaring of the VHF radio. This time it was different. My dreams went on and on, from one bizarre situation to the next, much longer than they should have. The last one, the dream I woke from, was about my sister and the glass float. Maddie and I were beachcombing together when she discovered it. We dug it out, and as soon as we did, a sea lion appeared just offshore, barking.

"He wants to play!" my little sister cried, and then she did the last thing I would have guessed. She threw our prize to the sea lion. The lion immediately started playing with the ball, pushing it back and forth with its snout, disappearing and then breaching high in the air, the ball flying even higher. This was a Steller's, a big bull, easily ten feet long. Maddie was clapping her hands and laughing. I was yelling, "He's not going to give it back!"

"Sure he will," Maddie said, and just then the sea lion took off with it. Out past the kelp beds the animal stopped, faced us, tossed the ball up in the air, and seemed to beckon with a flipper. Before I even knew what had happened, Maddie was swimming out to the sea lion, in the freezing cold water. Not only that, she was being swept out to sea by a riptide.

"Maddie!" I screamed. I jumped in and swam after her, knowing it meant both of us would drown. In an instant, the riptide took me, the land was vanishing, Maddie was calling. I couldn't see her; I was all wrapped in kelp and it was strangling me as surely as an octopus. I was going down.

I got so frightened I woke myself up.

And discovered sunshine spilling down the ladder.

My watch said it was 7:15 A.M. All confused, I threw off my sleeping bag and climbed the stairs.

Where was Tor? Why hadn't he woken me? What about the storm, the storm that had been brewing?

I found him on his bunk, sound asleep.

I looked over the bow. The ocean, thank goodness, was calm, but it was an eerie, dead calm. There wasn't a boat in sight. The emptiness, the stillness, the silence, were terrifying.

I shook Tor's shoulder. He blinked himself awake and saw broad daylight. He looked panicky, which scared the daylights out of me. "The barometer," he said. "What's it reading?"

"Twenty-eight and a half."

"Read it again."

"Twenty-eight and a half!"

We both ran onto the deck. The sky was streaky and red like a river of spawning sockeyes. There wasn't a boat in sight. The Pacific was dead calm, holding its breath.

"God help us," Tor said. "We have to get out of here."

17

I WENT BELOW AND THREW my clothes and boots on. By the time I got back up, we were under way. Tor had us on a GPS course for Lituya Bay. I cleared every bit of loose gear out of the cockpit and snapped a tarp over it, so it wouldn't get swamped if we ran into big waves.

"Of all times for me to oversleep," Tor bellowed as I returned to the wheelhouse. He slammed his fist on the table, as if that would help. "It must have been those useless pills Grace gave me."

Torsen grabbed the tide table booklet. He studied it intensely, staring at one page and pulling at his beard. At last he set it aside.

"I take it the tide needs to be high for us to be able to get into Lituya," I said.

"That's right, you have to go into the bay on the flood. If the tide is ebbing, you can't get in there."

"Is the current rushing out of the bay too strong? Too strong for this boat?"

"That's part of it. At the peak of the ebb, it can run twelve knots. You remember me telling you about the entrance, about the slot between the breakers? At high tide that gate is a hundred yards wide, but at low tide— shallower water—it closes shut. The surf breaks all the way across."

"Is it like you were talking about, crossing the bar into the Columbia River?"

"Same idea. You've got to cross that bar. Even at high tide, especially when it's windy, it can be tricky to get inside Lituya."

Tor punched in KRU-55 out of Yakutat. The weather forecast would be coming up in a few minutes.

No longer was the sea dead calm. A breeze was blowing out of the southeast, and that wasn't good. That's the direction most of the big blows come from. They're spawned out in the north Pacific, and by the time they reach the Gulf of Alaska, they're churning with a powerful counterclockwise rotation. The arms that fly off them curl around and attack from the southeast. "So where do we stand with the tides right now?" I asked. "Are we on high or low?"

"Look it up for yourself!"

"I will," I said, and reached for the tide tables.

Torsen eyed me as I searched for the right table, then said, "We've got half an hour of low left. There'll be half an hour of slack, then six of high."

"Which means we've got seven hours to get inside the bay. We need to be there by two-thirty this afternoon. Is that possible?"

"Weather depending."

"There must be some other spot we can run to."

"Cape Fairweather, but it's fifteen miles up the coast from Lituya. If we had drifted north last night instead of south, I'd be thinking about the cape, even though it's a lousy windbreak compared to Lituya Bay. But if we set a course for Fairweather right now, and the weather comes up, we'd be exposed a lot longer."

"We might not get there."

"You wanted to know. Now, do you feel better?"

The radio was beginning to spit out the weather forecast. They started with the Dixon Entrance, south of Prince of Wales Island. "Winds light to variable, with patches of sunshine."

My hopes began to rise. We were going to luck out. Our barometer indicated we must be close to a bad storm cell, but our seas weren't bad at all. The storm cell must be heading in some other direction.

As the forecast moved north, so did the wind speeds being reported. At last it was our turn: "Cape Spencer to Yakutat," the radio blared, "small craft warnings."

"Now they tell us," Tor said.

"Tor, we're forty-six miles from shore."

"I know, I know."

Minutes later, the first swell rolled ominously underneath us. It had come from the southeast.

The captain tuned the radio to Channel 16, the hailing channel used for emergencies, then switched to another, where fishermen were talking.

"I got up and tapped the glass at one-thirty," a skipper was saying. "It took such a drop I spooked and took off running. I got my sights on Cape Spencer. This could be some kind of blow."

"Roger that," said another. "Good thinking, getting a jump on it. The rest of us, at least we'll be snug inside Lituya before long."

Tor turned the volume down. "We're kind of out on a limb," I couldn't help saying. "The storm better spin off in some other direction."

"This bird can fly in foul weather. The *Storm Petrel* has lived up to her name in more than a few blows. Plus, you've got a seafaring Norwegian at the wheel. That ought to count for something."

The resolve in Torsen's weathered face made me momentarily thankful that he was such an ornery piece of work.

For three hours, we made eight knots. The bow kept lifting higher and the swells came more frequently, but we were making good time. I did the math. We had come twenty-eight miles and had eighteen left to go, with four hours left before Lituya's entrance closed. To get there with a cushion, at 2:00 P.M., with a half hour left of high tide, all we had to average was five knots.

Just as I began to breathe easier, the wind struck. Faster than I would have believed possible, it went from a breeze to thirty knots, and the sea was suddenly running with white horses. Out the wheelhouse windows, the sky to the southeast was turning a sickly blue-black. "How can it whip up this fast?" I asked.

"Just does," the captain replied.

The wind was gusting to fifty knots now. Tor's big troller didn't feel so big. The *Storm Petrel* was beginning to heel over on her beam ends. "Shut that half-door out to the deck," Tor ordered.

Spray was whipping off the sides of the boat and over the afterdeck. I closed the bottom half of the door, then returned to the table and looked out over the bucking bow. I did a double take at what I saw half around to starboard. To the southeast, a white wall of water stood up above the ocean. "Tsunami?" I asked, feeling sick and weightless.

"Look closer. That's a whole bunch of waves, driven by the storm front."

"Coming our way, Tor."

"Yes, they are," he said calmly. He was standing tall, like a battlefield commander. I felt the bottom drop out of my stomach. The *Storm Petrel* couldn't retreat. Outrunning the wind, that was impossible.

Visibility dropped suddenly to half a mile. On came the wind-driven rain and the spindrift. It was getting so dark, so fast, I'd never seen anything like it. "Kid," Tor said urgently. "Everything that isn't nailed down in this wheelhouse, get it inside a cupboard or get it down below."

"Will do," I said. I went to work in the galley first. Then I cleared the tabletop.

"My bunk. The bag and the mattress and everything. Stow it below."

I stuffed Torsen's loose clothes and his sleeping bag into his duffel. Once down the ladder, I wedged it into the bunk opposite mine. I went back up for the mattress, grabbed it, and found myself looking at the Russian plaques. "What about the plaques, Tor? What should I do with them?"

"If they fly around, they could take our heads off. Put 'em at the bottom of the closet across from the fire extinguisher, or on the floor of the john."

Fast as I could, I stowed everything that had to be stowed. "Thirty seconds," I heard Tor call. I threw the loose silverware and the dishes into drawers, and I slid into position at the table in time to brace myself for the first wave.

"Hang on!" Tor yelled.

The first one came down on us like a falling building. I was amazed that the front windows didn't blow out. Then came more waves. Water hit the windows like gravel, forcing itself inside through every seam.

"How do you like this, Billy?" a crackling voice on the radio asked.

"I'll like it a whole lot better when we're inside the bay," another voice answered.

With the seas blowing, it was impossible to see more than fifty yards ahead. On the crests of the waves, the wind caught us full and forced the bow sideways. Tor responded every time by cranking hard on the wheel and goosing the throttle. It took a full burst of power for the rudder to swing us back into the waves and the wind.

A gust slammed us amidships, and the *Petrel* nearly lay over on her side. I had a death grip on the tabletop. "What does the wind gauge say?" I yelled over the shriek of the wind.

"Seventy knots."

"That's eighty miles an hour. Ever been in a storm this bad?"

"Never. Let's hope it doesn't get worse."

It did. We were taking a horrible beating. Tor had to fight to stay in the seat behind the wheel.

When I didn't think it could get any worse, a wave bigger than the rest reared up and came down hard, right on top of the wheelhouse. Tor was thrown to the floor. His books went flying out of their spill-proof shelves, the ceiling was raining salt water, cabinet doors flew open. Canned goods rolled out onto the floor, glass was breaking, water was hissing on the stove top, charts were thrown everywhere, and then came a crash from down in the engine room. We were spinning in the surf, totally out of control.

18

T OR PICKED HIMSELF UP and climbed back into the captain's chair. The boat had been spun so far around, we were quartering before the wind instead of into it. Still in motion, we were about to be hit broadside by the next big wave. With wheel and throttle, Torsen added to the *Storm Petrel*'s momentum instead of trying to reverse it, and gave the wave our butt end.

The *Petrel*'s stern took the brunt of the wave squarely. The wave rolled over the back rail and washed across the deck. If the cockpit hadn't been tarped, it would have filled, and the boat would have become hopelessly back heavy.

"Should I clean up all this mess in the wheel-house?" I shouted over the whine of the wind.

"Forget about that for now. Go below and see what came loose."

I was trembling. I had turned to jelly. Get ahold of yourself, I thought, or you're not going to get through this.

It all felt too big. Huge. Hopeless.

I lurched to the galley sink and threw up. It wasn't seasickness, it was stark terror.

"Quitter!" Torsen screamed. "Just like I thought, you're nothing but a quitter!"

I heaved some more, wiped my face with a dishrag, and held on tight, or I would have been thrown to the floor. How much punishment could the boat take?

"Engine's overheating—get down there now!"

He was right, it had to be done. I waded through the clutter on the floor, spun, and went down the ladder.

It was raining from the engine room ceiling, the motor hissing with every drop. The bilge bump was loud and sucking full bore, but couldn't keep up. The floor was ankle-deep in water. Bracing as best I could, afraid I'd be thrown onto steaming hot metal, I sloshed around trying to figure out what was wrong.

It was easy enough to see that the auxiliary generator for the lights had broken loose from its mounts, which would explain the crash we'd heard, but not the engine overheating.

My mind shut down as it hit me: if we capsize while I'm down here, I'm dead for sure.

My stomach was cramping again. This time I fought it off and battled to get myself under control. Suddenly I saw it—the auxiliary generator had fallen onto a cooling hose. The hose had been nearly pinched shut.

I got down on one knee and lifted the generator off the engine, then made sure the hose hadn't stayed pinched flat. It was back in working order, circulating water and coolant.

Lurching around, I found a piece of rope and secured the auxiliary generator so it couldn't fly around and damage wiring, cooling hoses, carburation, any vital system. If the engine went down, we had no chance.

Something was strange about the exhaust stack. It had turned from black to white with all the salt water running down it. Thank goodness our leaks were above the hull. Thank goodness the hull was fiberglass, not old wooden planks like the hull of the *Chimes*.

Topside, I discovered that Torsen had somehow turned us around and back into the wind. My eyes went to the temperature gauge. It was nearly back to normal. "Seawater's forcing its way through the exhaust stack's roof jack," I reported.

Torsen waved my news off like it was nothing. "We lost the hatch."

"What hatch?"

"The hatch over the fish hold. That hundred pound fiberglass cover, gone with the wind. I saw it blow away."

This was sickening news. The belly of the boat was

open to the sea. "Is the hold's bilge pump working?" I shouted above the whine of the wind.

"It's working, but the radio's not."

"Why not?"

"The antenna broke clean off."

"We can't call Mayday?"

"That's right, we can't. Tell me, do we have anything we can lash the plaques to? What do we have that floats?"

"The little skiff and the life raft up top, but we can't get to them."

"Skiff's gone—I saw it fly. You didn't tie it down very good."

"Thanks for sharing," I said.

He ignored me. "I don't want the plaques loose. Think, what do we have that we can attach them to?"

"You think we're going to capsize?"

"I didn't say that. I need you to take care of those plaques. Do it, and do it now!"

This was too much. "Why should I help you save them?" I hollered.

"Don't you understand how important those are? They can't be lost!"

"*You* don't understand! You're just going to sell them anyway, I know you are. They'll be lost either way. They should be in a museum and you know it!"

"Quit arguing and help me!"

"I have an idea," I shouted. I balanced my way out the back door to the deck. The hatch cover was gone, but the plywood tray still spanned the opening. In a gully between waves, I grabbed one of the plastic milk crates, the one I'd used for stashing the big glass fishing float for my sister. The glass ball had been a snug fit, and was still inside.

I had to wait out a big pitch and roll before I made my move for the wheelhouse. Once inside, I took the glass ball out and placed the plaques on the bottom of the crate, one atop the other. Then I put the float back inside. To keep the ball from floating out of the crate, all I needed was rope. There was a coil in the closet behind me.

Tying to one of the built-in handles on the crate, I lashed the rope over the top of the ball and back and forth and every which way through the plastic ribbing until only glimpses of the green glass could be seen among the lashings. I tied off to the opposite handle with a slew of half hitches. "Done," I called out.

"Good," Torsen replied. "Here comes another big one. Hang on!"

I braced for all I was worth, and even so, was nearly thrown onto the stove. The *Petrel* heeled over so far she was on her side. Out the side window, I saw the port trolling pole disappear underwater. I thought for sure the whole boat would follow.

Miraculously, the *Petrel* righted herself, but something was wrong outside. One heavy thud was followed by another. "Did it break?" Torsen called. "Did the pole break off?"

I craned my neck to see. "No, the pole flew up against the mast. But it's not in its bracket."

"The port stabilizer! What happened to the stabilizer?"

"It must be up against the hull."

"It'll punch a hole in it."

"Why didn't you pull them this morning?" I yelled. "We could've gone faster."

"For stability, fool! I didn't know it would get this bad. We have to pull 'em now. The one against the hull, you should be able to reach out and cut its rope."

"You gotta be kidding, Tor. You go out there."

"My back won't let me, or I would. Listen, kid, you have to tighten the stays on that port pole so the pole stays upright. If it flops back down, its rigging is going to end up in the prop or the rudder, and then we're done. The starboard pole, you gotta pull it vertical and cut its stabilizer loose."

This was it. This was the opportunity he'd been waiting for. I could read it behind his eyes, cold as the eyes on the octopus, years before, that had tried to drag me into the sea. "Dream on," I yelled at him. "You go out there!"

"Fine, we'll go down together. That stabilizer is like a spear point, you know it and I know it. The hull's an inch and a half thick. You give that some thought."

"Not without a survival suit."

"Go get the suits, then."

"There's only one, remember?"

"Go get it!" he thundered.

I went below and came back with it. I kicked my boots off and began to pull on the one-piece suit. It had a nylon shell that was lined with closed-cell foam to float you and buffer you from the freezing seawater. I zippered it shut and adjusted the neoprene cuffs, then pulled my boots back on. I put on rubber gloves, grabbed a sharp knife from a galley drawer, and sloshed my way to the half-door, which I fastened open. I jammed my body in the doorframe, awed by the mountainous, wind-driven seas all around the back of the boat. How was I going to do what had to be done and stay on board?

The immediate problem was crossing to the port rail without being thrown into the yawning hatch, where salmon that had spilled over the tops of the side bins littered the central floor.

With an eye on the waves, I timed my move, keeping tight against the back of the wheelhouse. It didn't take long to snake my way around the corner to the base of the port pole. I wrapped my legs around it, reached out with the knife to cut the stabilizer rope, and nearly went over when the boat pitched suddenly in the direction I was leaning. But I managed to hang on, and then I sawed the rope in two. The stabilizer was on its way to the bottom of the Pacific.

Just then a wave slammed the *Petrel* from the opposite side, and the port pole fell from vertical back to its fishing position. I was going to have to haul it up by hand.

Which I did, all the while barely hanging on. The wind lashed like a whip, the waves poured over the side of the boat, and salt water stung like fire in my eyes. At last I had the port pole upright and its rigging so tight and double-knotted, it couldn't go anywhere. I grabbed the knife, which I had stuck in the side of the wheelhouse, then crabbed my way around the back to the starboard side.

In the time it had taken me to get the port side taken care of, the starboard pole had bent like a straw. The stays and the rigging were a tangled mess. I heaved on the line with all my might, but nothing gave. With the boat pitching every which way, I got back into the wheelhouse and told Torsen where we stood.

"Go back and try again," he ordered.

"What do I do different?" I asked in total frustration.

"Pull harder!"

"Look, I pulled as hard as I could. Just leave it be."

"You don't know what it'll do to us. Here, get behind the wheel, I'll do it myself. When in doubt, give it throttle."

"Take the suit, Tor. Here, I'll take it off."

He ignored me, just took the knife and pushed past.

There was nothing to do but grab hold of the wheel spokes, fight for control of the rudder, push on the throttle, and face the waves. A glance over my shoulder confirmed that Torsen was already outside. I remembered to monitor our direction of travel on the GPS. Unless we stayed on course for Lituya Bay and got there in time, there was no way out of this for either of us.

This was a nightmare, a never-ending ride on a crazed whale. I prayed I wouldn't have to face a wave like the one that crashed down on the wheelhouse.

I had no vision of the spot where Torsen was working. At last, over my shoulder, I caught a glimpse of the starboard pole cranking up against the mast. Somehow Torsen had jerked it loose. Now he just had to finish— tie it off and cut the stabilizer free.

The wind began to shriek louder than ever. Here came a wave as big as any we'd seen. I pointed the bow straight into it and leaned hard on the throttle. The wave was so tall, it looked like we might not be able to climb it. I had the sickening feeling we were slipping back. If we did, we would broach, swamp, and capsize.

We barely made it over the top, but as we cleared the crest, the prop lost its bite. This time we slipped sideways. When the prop caught again, it was all I could do in the face of yet another giant wave to crank furiously on the wheel, come about, and run with the wind.

I was running with that wave, on its very crest, and looking down into an abyss. The bottom of the trough seemed a hundred feet below. When in doubt, Torsen had said, give it throttle. That's what I did, I slammed the throttle forward. In a heartbeat we would hit bottom, and when we did, we had to be in control, or we'd be tossed around like a toy.

It was a rough landing. At the bottom of the trough,

the *Petrel* yawed badly, then broached immediately to windward. I was thrown out of my seat. My head cracked against something. I thought for sure we had capsized.

Amazingly, as I struggled to my feet, the *Storm Petrel* was righting herself. One of our poles—the starboard pole—was in the water. It had broken clean off before Tor could secure it.

There was something else in the water, amid the heaving gray seas: the bearded face and upraised hand of Torsen. He'd been swept overboard.

19

I PULLED BACK ON THE throttle and took the boat out of gear. I ran to the deck, hung on tight, and tried to spot Tor. He was on a rising wave a hundred feet away, floundering in the surf, trying to swim.

There had to be something I could throw him, and fast. There wasn't a life ring, like on the *Chimes*. What, what else was there? All I could think of was the milk crate with the glass float. I grabbed it from the closet. This was going to be a crying shame, throwing the plaques into the sea.

For a second I hesitated. Wasn't he exactly where he had wanted me to be?

Torsen was still struggling to stay on the surface. I got his attention, then heaved the crate as far as I could.

I waited, the *Petrel* getting slammed, as Torsen swam after it, up and down the slopes of the waves. He struggled, until at last he had hold of the crate. It was buoyant enough to give him some relief, but by this time he was well behind the boat and nearly out of sight.

I ran back inside and got the *Petrel* turned around. By the time the bow was pointing to the area where I guessed he was, Torsen was nowhere to be seen. What now?

I just had to make my best guess and hope I was right.

There he was, to starboard, arms encircling the rope-wrapped fishing float. I steered in his direction, wondering how I was going to get him aboard. A ninety-pound salmon had nearly been too much for me.

I brought the *Petrel* close, then took it out of gear again. The boat tossed every which way. I raced to the deck, hoping I could get to him before a crashing wave got to the boat.

"Over here, over here!" came Torsen's voice, this time from the port side.

I crabbed across to his side of the boat, desperate to avoid being pitched over myself. I got down on hands and knees and went to the rail. Tor had the crate clutched tightly to his chest.

"Get closer," I screamed. "Give me your hand!"

He sidestroked closer, a wild look in his eye. "Won't work!" he yelled. "Get a gaff hook! I'll grab it!"

One eye on the spilling seas, I scrambled for a gaff, then shimmied back on my belly.

Torsen was trying his best to stay close to the boat as his strength drained. He was blue in the face. I reached as far as I could with the gaff hook; he kicked and was able to grab it with his right hand.

"On the count of three," I heard him yell. "I'll kick, you pull."

I rose as I counted "One—two—*three!*" I pulled with all my strength.

I heard him kick. I heard him grunt. He managed to get one hand up on the bulwark, but it was futile. The wave dropped out from under him, and he was swept away.

The crate with the glass ball was swept away with him. Torsen appeared to glimpse it, and swam after it. Then he must have lost sight of it; I couldn't see it either. Tor gave up on it, turned, and swam back to the *Petrel*. "Use a rising wave," he cried over the shriek of the storm. "Gaff me in the shoulder blade!"

It was almost too horrible to imagine, but maybe he was right and it was his only chance of getting back on board.

The seas were building again toward another crescendo of fury, and Torsen was forced under. Just when I was sure he was gone, he reappeared farther away, and struggled once more toward my side of the boat.

Here he came, arm over arm, and here came the rising wave he wanted. I watched the seas closely, spotted my chance, and stood up full height. I leaned over and gaffed Tor behind his shoulder, sticking the hook deep. All in the same motion, I pulled as hard as I possibly could, both hands on the gaff handle, and threw myself backward. Torsen, kicking and floundering like a big yellowfin tuna, teetered close to the balance point on the bulwark. He was nearly halfway into the boat. Just then, the wave fell out from underneath him. The boat rocked in his direction, and I felt myself flying toward him and the swallowing sea.

"Let go!" he screamed. I did, and not a moment too soon. Torsen fell, as if down a mountain slope, into a yawning gulf, and went under.

It was Tor's warning and the sudden recoil of the *Petrel* that saved me from going in with him. At the point of no return, gravity swung in my favor, and I was able to stop my momentum.

My last glimpse of Tor Torsen saw him giving up the fight, slipping under the waves. His precious Russian plaques were nowhere to be seen. The troller took another heavy hit, and suddenly I was flying backward, with nothing to break my fall, into a void that turned out to be the fish hold. I would have broken my neck if I hadn't landed on the salmon that had spilled over the bin boards.

I climbed out and clawed my way into the wheelhouse. The *Petrel* was a cork in a maelstrom. It was only by a combination of superior boat design and luck that the *Petrel* hadn't capsized. It might yet, that was all too obvious. As I lurched toward the captain's chair behind the wheel, a tremendous wave broke on the bow and blew out the forward window to my left in an explosion of glass and water. I was thrown to the floor. A torrent of water poured down on me, and the wind was howling.

I got up, climbed into the seat, and reached for the controls. I put the boat in gear and opened up the throttle, then hung on to the spokes of the wheel with all my might.

More throttle, I needed more throttle. The rudder responded, and I was able to point the bow into the weather and regain something like control.

I searched for Tor as long as I dared, knowing I had to race the clock to Lituya Bay. *Why didn't you put on the survival suit,* I kept asking.

A sudden lull in the storm seemed like a screaming signal that I better break and run for it. I got back on the GPS course for Lituya, pushing the *Petrel* toward land at full throttle.

The seas were rough, but nothing like they had been. For a good long while, I was able to average seven knots. The sky, however, was turning terribly dark to the southeast again. I had to gain every inch I could, and sneak into the bay before the next arm of the storm arrived in full force. I couldn't see the coast but I knew I had to be near. Nine miles, said the GPS, with ninety minutes to get there before high tide ended at 2:30.

Two miles off the bay, at two o'clock, the new storm front struck. I had to steer manually; the autopilot couldn't respond fast enough. Seas fell on the troller like avalanches. The wind gauge was reading a steady ninety, with gusts over a hundred knots. Another window broke under the barrage. More wind and water rushed in. I had the panicky feeling I'd be swimming real soon.

The wheelhouse was in shambles. The electronics were still working, the satellite still tracking my position relative to the mouth of the bay. I kept watching the map on the monitor. I had to keep my direction of travel arrow pointed at the mouth of the bay, or I'd never get there. *If we capsize, take a deep breath while there's time. Remember where the door is. Get out fast, and swim free, and get to the surface.*

"Two miles!" I cried. "Two crummy miles!"

Eyes constantly shifting from the seas to the navigation monitor, I steered and worked the throttle. It was moment to moment trying to adjust to the onslaught.

Time was my enemy, as much as the storm. In the next forty-five minutes, it was all I could do to gain a mile. Two-thirty, the target, had sickeningly come and gone. There was only fifteen minutes left of the slack tide.

I kept staring into the dark rain and flying spindrift as I battled closer. Land was close, but I couldn't see it. What I did see, suddenly, was an almost continuous line of breaking waves. In the center, there was a hole, the narrowest of slots. The entrance to Lituya Bay?

The channel through the bar? The gate?

The instruments said I was only half a mile off the bay. On the left-hand side, behind the waves, I thought I saw a line of spindly trees. I didn't know for sure, but I had to believe they were growing along the spit Torsen had described, the narrow neck of land on the north side of the bottleneck entrance to the bay.

Yes, I could see it all now, the spit on the left, the breaking waves in front of the bottleneck, the land on the right. I was looking at the mouth of Lituya Bay.

I checked my watch. The slack between tides was over. The tide was ebbing; water was beginning to pour out of the bay. I'd come too late.

My forearms were cramping but I hung tight to the wheel as the storm threatened to drive the *Petrel* back to sea. Before the slot closed, I had to go for it. There was no giving up on Lituya Bay. Trying to make it to Cape Fairweather at the height of the storm would be suicidal.

I stayed on course, never taking my eyes off the slot in the line of ferocious breakers. With every minute, the entrance was shrinking.

Then, right before my eyes, the gate closed. The gap was gone. The huge white surf was breaking continuously across the bar. What now?

If I tried to punch through at the beginning of low tide, and hung up on the sand bar with the surf much more powerful than normal and the hold uncovered, the *Petrel* would be swamped in a hurry, then broken to bits.

Surf more powerful than normal . . . did that change things? Could the storm surge, all that wind-driven water piling onto the coast, provide me enough extra water to work with, to float me high enough and push me on through without being immobilized by the current rushing out of the bay? It was a desperate theory.

Out of nowhere, my last morning in Protection came back to me, so real I could hear the fire crackling in the stove. I saw the floathouse suddenly pitch up in the air, saw the sugar bowl sail across the table, saw my dad reach out to grab it and miss. There we were, running out onto the deck, laughing, in time to see the whale come out from underneath. "It's a good sign for Robbie fishing the big water," Maddie had said.

"We'll soon find out, Maddie." I laughed out loud as I aimed the bow of the *Storm Petrel* for the violent entrance of Lituya Bay, at the same angle that the storm was sending its huge swells against the bar. I made sure my survival suit was zipped up as far as it would go.

I thought of Tor at the last, when his weight was pulling me into the ocean, how he'd told me to let go. He was done, and he knew it. Whatever terrible thoughts he'd been thinking since he first met me, the last thing on his mind had been that he wanted me to live.

"I aim to," I said aloud. "Your *Petrel* and your deckhand have made it this far."

I eased back on the throttle. I felt a big lump roll under the boat, then another and another. Some of the swells were bigger than others.

"Gotta pick the right one," I shouted above the whine of the wind.

Over my shoulder, I spotted the swell I wanted. It was rising, rising, rising, and I wasn't going to let it slide underneath me. I gunned the *Petrel* full throttle, and the troller plunged ahead with the swell. I was committed. When this enormous wave broke onto the current shooting out of the bay, the collision was going to be colossal. If the *Petrel* foundered, I had to bail out fast. The ocean would make short work of her.

"Hang on," I told myself. "It won't be long." I stood up, spread my feet wide, and clung to the spokes of the wheel with my hands clenched tight as talons. The boat came off the crest of the wave in free fall, mountains of water on both sides, and it hit bottom with a thud. The troller shuddered, and I was sure it was the end.

It was all white water and confusion. For the time being, we were intact. It seemed possible that the hull had withstood the impact. The propeller was still responding and so was the rudder. We must have bounced loose off the bottom. I had a death grip on the wheel—the turbulence was all but overwhelming—and was cranking it hard left to keep the boat from being spun into the whirlpools.

Next thing I knew, the *Storm Petrel* was being sucked into the backwash. Over my shoulder, the next wave was building higher and higher and was about to break. I pointed the nose of the *Petrel* directly into the current and slammed the throttle forward. The boat began to gain against the current. Relative to the trees on the spit, directly opposite, she was making headway.

How much headway, that was the question. The tremendous wave looming above the *Petrel* was about to break on her back. "Go, go!" I screamed. The wave broke behind us instead of on top of us. Its surge gave an assist, adding enough water and momentum to allow her to slip inside the bay, taking me along for the ride.

Suddenly I saw trollers, dozens of trollers anchored inside Lituya Bay.

They must have been watching. They all started blowing their foghorns.

As I motored into the bay, my eyes filled with tears, and I gave a few blasts in return.

20

ONCE INSIDE THE BAY, I steered for the nearest troller. I brought the *Storm Petrel* as close as possible to the *Slow and Easy*, whose skipper appeared on the deck. We were only a stone's throw apart but had to holler back and forth over the wind. At last he understood me. I moved a little farther off and dropped anchor while he lowered his skiff to come and get me. I was soon inside his wheelhouse, on the radio, reporting Tor's disappearance.

Tor wasn't the only one missing. In the last hour, two trollers had sunk trying to make it to Cape Fairweather. Both had been able to broadcast Mayday calls before they went down. Two Coast Guard helicopter teams with swimmers were attempting their rescue with the storm still raging.

"You're lucky to be alive," the skipper of the *Slow and Easy* told me. "Lucky you gambled on Lituya and lucky you made it across the bar."

Doug Fender, one of the many solo skippers this king season, was happy to have company. He'd been sixteen days alone and looked pretty haggard, still covered with salmon scales. In his mirror, I looked worse. Fender made a slumgullion stew—some canned stuff with onions, carrots, and potatoes thrown in—and we listened to the radio as we ate. The trollers in the bay were all comparing notes about the storm. Everyone was anxious to hear the fate of the missing fishermen.

It wasn't long before we heard that the skipper of the *Trumpeter*, along with his deckhand, had been rescued by the Coast Guard swimmers. They'd been found in their life raft, both wearing survival suits. Torsen and the skipper of the *Distant Thunder* were still missing.

I asked Fender where Tor's body might wash up. He described a tide rip a few miles north that collected most of the flotsam and jetsam along that stretch of coast. The weather forecast described the storm as fast moving. There was a good chance it would be over by sunrise.

The trollers in Lituya Bay were making plans to cross the bar in the morning, before high tide ended and the entrance closed. I was asleep aboard the *Storm Petrel* by a quarter to eight, counting on a borrowed alarm clock to wake me.

At six the next morning I woke to the fresh memory of the storm, scenes on a scale too huge and terrible to be believed, yet it had all happened: the violence of the water, Tor in the ocean without a survival suit, me trying to gaff him like a salmon. These were images that were never going to go away.

I climbed the ladder into the emptiness of the wheelhouse. With his equipment and possessions all around me—much of it still on the floor—Torsen's absence loomed large. I shuddered remembering him going down at the last, his acceptance of it.

I went out onto the deck to see if the weather was going to pin me down for another day.

The storm was gone. I could see the forest surrounding the bay, the island at its center, the glaciers at its head, and all the way up the great white wall. Jagged peaks were shining in the morning light.

Fender came onto his deck and told me the news. His voice carried easily across the still water. The two missing skippers were still unaccounted for. I dreaded the inevitable: I would have to contact Tor's daughter as soon as possible.

I crossed the bar in the *Storm Petrel* at the next high tide, while the going was good, along with the small fleet of trollers that had sheltered in Lituya Bay. Once on the ocean, the trollers headed south. King season was over, and they were eager to sell. Almost all of them were heading to the closest fish plant, at Pelican.

I wanted to sell as much as any of them. Wanted more, even, to get home. Once out of the bay, though, I turned north. It wasn't only Torsen's body I was looking for, it was the milk crate and the plaques.

I heard a helicopter but I couldn't see it. No doubt they'd been searching all night.

By the time I reached the tide rip, there were trollers on the horizon that were heading my way. These were the boats that had sheltered at Cape Fairweather. They would be abreast of my position in half an hour. I had thirty minutes to look, and then I would join them for the run down to Pelican.

It was tricky guiding the *Storm Petrel* alongside the rip. It was swirling with opposing currents, awash with kelp and other debris that could foul the propeller. I was afraid I might actually find Torsen's body, all swathed in kelp. Finding the crate seemed impossible. All that rope I had used to secure the big glass float inside the crate was the same shade of brown as the bull kelp. I kept telling myself to look for the roundness of the ball camouflaged by the rope. That was the only thing that would give it away.

I had passed back and forth along the rip half a dozen times, as slowly as possible, and was close to giving up when a pair of sea otters caught my eye. They were playing in the rafts of kelp unmoored by the storm. I thought I saw a third otter, then realized it wasn't moving in any direction, just washing back and forth with the swells.

The third otter was the prize I was looking for. I soon had it on board, none the worse for wear: the big green fishing float for my sister, the Russian plaques for history.

*　*　*

Two weeks later, I met up with Torsen's daughter. Grace came to Port Protection and stayed with my family. She'd come to arrange for the sale of the *Storm Petrel*, which my father and I had brought home from Pelican at her request.

I didn't know what to expect. How had she taken the news of her father's death? What would she think of me? She had said almost nothing when I called her with the grim news.

When Moose Borden brought her in the air taxi and she first stepped onto the deck of our floathouse, tears came to her eyes and to mine. "And so we meet, Robbie Daniels," she said. "I've brought the journal, Rezanov's journal. It was in my father's safe-deposit box. Thank you so much for telling me about it."

The first low tide that came along, Grace and I went for a slow walk around the cove. "Ever since he lost my mother," she began, "my father has been a difficult man."

I was surprised by how quickly she had cut to the chase, and I didn't know quite how to respond.

"I'll bet he was hard to work for," she said with a smile.

"We had our ups and downs."

"Tell me about the storm," she said, "and how he died."

I told her about Tor going out to secure the starboard trolling pole, getting swept over, how I threw him the crate with the glass ball and the plaques. I spared no detail, not even the gaff hook. It was what happened at the last, Tor saving my life by warning me to let go, that gave her the comfort she was looking for. Grace appreciated everything I told her about her father—especially that he'd talked of her and her mother.

"What should I do with the plaques and the journal?" she asked.

"There's a museum in Sitka that has the first plaque ever found. I think your plaques and the journal belong in that museum, since Sitka was the capital of Russian Alaska."

"Then that's where they'll go. Meanwhile, I have some settling up to do with you."

Back at the floathouse, Grace wrote me a check for my fifteen percent of the take from the two fish sales, the small one to the *Angie* and the big one to Pelican Seafoods. It came to $2,256, far more than I'd ever hoped to make in one king season.

From Protection we all went to Sitka in the *Storm Petrel*, its blown-out windows and the radio antenna freshly replaced. Once we tied up, we headed straight for the Bishop's House Museum. My family and I were proud to be there with Grace, to be a part of it, when she presented the plaques and the journal on behalf of her father. It turned out that Tor Torsen was going to be famous instead of infamous, in spite of himself.

On the way back to Protection, I was at the wheel and the other four were at the table as we skirted the tide rips off of Cape Ommaney. Grace got up and looked out the wheelhouse window at the drama of the surf pounding the tip of the cape. "It doesn't matter if my father's body is never found," she said softly. "In a way, it would be fitting if the sea, which he loved so much, took him to be with my mother."

There was a silence, and then Maddie said, "Your father fished on the prettiest boat there ever was."

Grace turned around and smiled. "I know, Maddie, and I've been thinking. I sure hate to sell the *Petrel* to strangers."

It took a few seconds for this to sink in. "We could never afford her," my father said. "She's not in the same class with our *Chimes of Freedom*."

Grace's eyes, a deep sea green like her father's, were all lit up. "What if we were simply to exchange boats straight across? I'm certain my father would have liked that."

My mother gasped. "We couldn't—"

"No, really," Grace said. "I'd like to be able to picture you all together on the *Petrel*, just like now."

I was still trying to get ahold of what she was saying. This was huge.

But was it true, like she'd said, that Tor would have wanted me to end up with his boat? I searched for a memory. Suddenly I could see him hanging on the hayrack and watching me pull king salmon. I could almost hear his gruff voice saying, "Not bad for a morning's work."

So many things came flooding back: the dawn colors our first day out, all four lines rattling, the two of us pulling salmon side by side, the roll of the open ocean, the stone-washed beauty of the capes. Our feelings for the trolling life were one and the same, and Tor had known that. The rest of it, the dark parts of our journey, I wanted to put behind me, let it all drop to the bottom of the Pacific. Maybe Grace was right, that this was what her father would have wanted.

My mother got up and stood next to Grace. They were both looking over the bow into the distance. "We could fish the outside waters off Addington and Chirikof, right from home," my mother said. "It would be a big addition to our economy to be able to fish king season, and it would mean college money for Robbie and Maddie."

"Let's ask the man at the wheel," my father said. "What do you say, Robbie? You're the one with the experience on the outside waters."

"As long as we keep land in sight," I said. "Count me in."

I was already thinking that I wouldn't have to wait until next year's king season to show my family the wonders of Cape Addington. In a couple of weeks, the cohos would be running strong out there.

These outside waters were in my blood now. It

would be a while before I felt okay about taking the *Petrel* out as far as Tor and I had gone, but I knew there would come a day when I'd point her bow back toward the Fairweather Grounds. Maybe it's true that the trolling way of life is in its twilight years. But the twilight lasts a long, long time up here in Alaska, and I mean to enjoy every minute of it.

Author's Note

I've often mined my personal experience for fiction, but never so quickly as with *Leaving Protection*. I had been visiting southeast Alaska for years, but this story was a direct result of two visits in 2002, the first in May and the second in July.

In May my wife, Jean, and I visited historic sites in Sitka, the old Russian capital. I have a longtime interest in the history of Russian Alaska. From Sitka we traveled via Ketchikan to Prince of Wales Island and the town of Craig. Sitka and Craig are the foremost commercial fishing harbors among the outer islands of Southeast.

I was in Craig at the invitation of a teacher, Julie Yates. It was in Craig's harbor I first set foot on a salmon troller, her father's boat and her namesake, the *Julie Kristine*. I had long been captivated by these picturesque boats, and I told her that one of my great ambitions in life was to catch a king salmon. Julie suggested I should return one day and work with her and her dad on the *Julie Kristine*. I told her I would love to take her up on that. She added that I should write a novel about commercial fishing. I said that sounded like a great idea, but I would like to go fishing whether or not it led to a story.

Little did I know how soon I would be working aboard that boat. In June, a forest fire closed the wilderness close to my home in Colorado, where I'd been planning a backpacking trip. Late in the month, I called Julie up and asked if, by any chance, I might join her and her father that very summer. She talked with her father, George, and called right back. "Hop on a plane," she told me. "King season starts the first of July."

By pure luck, I got in on the best king salmon season in many years. Julie and her father returned from their first outing with eight hundred kings, plus half as many cohos. I joined them for their second and third trips, seven days of fishing combined.

Every day, we were up at 4 A.M. and fished until 8 P.M. My primary job was to clean the fish and ice them in the hold, and that kept me plenty busy. Still, I had time to appreciate the beauty. We fished a mile or two off Cape Addington and Cape Chirikof. I was having the time of my life, and was beginning to wonder if I might be able to think up a fishing story that would put my readers on a salmon troller, too.

In his fourth decade trolling for salmon, George Yates was ever patient with my greenhorn questions, both on the boat and afterward. In addition to George and Julie, I would like to thank others on Prince of Wales Island who provided considerable assistance and inspiration. The Castle brothers, Brian and Kevin, teachers and commercial fishermen, provided hospitality and telephone consult, as did Julie's husband, Chad Fulton. Chad grew up partly at Port Protection. A jack of all trades from a young age, he commuted to school by himself in a skiff.

At the docks in Craig, I met the Sebastian family from Point Baker, an isolated fishing community near Port Protection. Joe and Joan, along with their children Forest and Elsa, inspired the Daniels family in my novel. The Sebastians fish the inside waters on their classic 1937 troller, the *Alta E.*

I returned home with an armful of books to add to my library on southeast Alaska. For months I immersed myself in the reading. By late fall I was writing. My early attempts at the novel died out. It was only when I remembered a plaque I'd seen in the Bishop's House in Sitka that I began to picture a way to make the fishing story into something more. The Russian possession plaques were the key, opening the door to a multilayered story. With the help of Sitka National Historical Park, I found their history in "Symbols of Russian America: Imperial Crests and Possession Plates in North America," by Mary Foster and Steve Henrickson, which appeared in the November 1991 issue of *Concepts*, a publication of the Alaska State Museums.

For readers looking for more detail on the Russians

in Alaska and Rezanov's saga, I would suggest the work of Hector Chevigny, author of *Russian America: The Great Alaskan Venture 1741–1867* and *Lost Empire: The Life and Adventures of Nikolai Rezanov* (both Binford & Mort Publishing, 1965). I would also recommend *Otter Skins, Boston Ships, and China Goods: The Maritime Fur Trade of the Northwest Coast, 1785–1841*, by James R. Gibson (McGill–Queen's University Press and University of Washington Press, 1992).

I would point readers who would like to learn more about salmon trolling to *Pacific Troller: Life on the Northwest Fishing Grounds* by Francis E. Caldwell (Trafford Publishing; first published by Alaska Northwest Books, 1978). Caldwell's book includes the fishery on the Fairweather Grounds and an account of the giant waves in Lituya Bay caused by the July 1958 earthquake, complete with photographs of the bay after the event.

Durango, Colorado
May 2003